"Merida," he said in a low, growly voice, and she lifted her face to hear what he had to say. **"Come to bed."**

He could see the heat spread on her cheeks and the rapid blink shutter her glittering eyes, but he did not retract or soften his invitation. Ethan wanted her very much. He had chosen to walk from the hospital for the chance of seeing her again.

For this.

"Ethan..." He saw the slight hesitation in her eyes and felt the sudden tension in her and then Merida spoke. "I haven't done this before."

And she *was* difficult to read, for he misread her then.

Not for a second did he consider that the woman in his arms, who knew how to sensually dance, who had kissed him back sexy and deep on the street, was a virgin.

"Come to bed, Merida."

Yes.

D1052594

One Night With Consequences

When one night...leads to pregnancy!

When succumbing to a night of unbridled desire, it's impossible to think past the morning after!

But with the sheets barely settled, that little blue line appears on the pregnancy test, and it doesn't take long to realize that one night of white-hot passion has turned into a lifetime of consequences!

Only one question remains:

How do you tell a man you've just met that you're about to share more than just his bed?

Find out in:

Claiming His Nine-Month Consequence by Jennie Lucas

Contracted for the Petrakis Heir by Annie West

Consequence of His Revenge by Dani Collins

Princess's Pregnancy Secret by Natalie Anderson

The Sheikh's Shock Child by Susan Stephens

The Italian's One-Night Consequence by Cathy Williams

Princess's Nine-Month Secret by Kate Hewitt

Consequence of the Greek's Revenge by Trish Morey

Look for more One Night With Consequences coming soon!

Carol Marinelli

———

THE INNOCENT'S SHOCK PREGNANCY

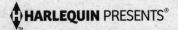

HARLEQUIN PRESENTS®

If you purchased this book without a cover you should be aware that this book is stolen property. It was reported as "unsold and destroyed" to the publisher, and neither the author nor the publisher has received any payment for this "stripped book."

Recycling programs for this product may not exist in your area.

ISBN-13: 978-1-335-41982-8

The Innocent's Shock Pregnancy

First North American publication 2018

Copyright © 2018 by Carol Marinelli

All rights reserved. Except for use in any review, the reproduction or utilization of this work in whole or in part in any form by any electronic, mechanical or other means, now known or hereafter invented, including xerography, photocopying and recording, or in any information storage or retrieval system, is forbidden without the written permission of the publisher, Harlequin Enterprises Limited, 22 Adelaide St. West, 40th Floor, Toronto, Ontario M5H 4E3, Canada.

This is a work of fiction. Names, characters, places and incidents are either the product of the author's imagination or are used fictitiously, and any resemblance to actual persons, living or dead, business establishments, events or locales is entirely coincidental.

This edition published by arrangement with Harlequin Books S.A.

For questions and comments about the quality of this book, please contact us at CustomerService@Harlequin.com.

® and TM are trademarks of Harlequin Enterprises Limited or its corporate affiliates. Trademarks indicated with ® are registered in the United States Patent and Trademark Office, the Canadian Intellectual Property Office and in other countries.

Printed in U.S.A.

www.Harlequin.com

Carol Marinelli recently filled in a form asking for her job title. Thrilled to be able to put down her answer, she put "writer." Then it asked what Carol did for relaxation and she put down the truth— "writing." The third question asked for her hobbies. Well, not wanting to look obsessed, she crossed her fingers and answered "swimming"—but, given that the chlorine in the pool does terrible things to her highlights, I'm sure you can guess the real answer!

Books by Carol Marinelli

Harlequin Presents

One Night With Consequences
The Sheikh's Baby Scandal

Secret Heirs of Billionaires
Claiming His Hidden Heir

Billionaires & One-Night Heirs
The Innocent's Secret Baby
Bound by the Sultan's Baby
Sicilian's Baby of Shame

Ruthless Royal Sheikhs
Captive for the Sheikh's Pleasure

The Billionaire's Legacy
Di Sione's Innocent Conquest

Visit the Author Profile page
at Harlequin.com for more titles.

CHAPTER ONE

'MERIDA! THANK GOODNESS you're here!'

Reece was clearly relieved as Merida stepped into the smart Fifth Avenue gallery.

A spring shower had chased her from the subway and, having dashed out of her apartment at short notice to get there, Merida hadn't brought an umbrella. Her long red curls were looking particularly wild, but there should be time to sort them before *he* arrived, she thought.

Merida Cartwright's smile was so bright and engaging no one would guess that stepping in at the last moment to give some VIP a private tour of the gallery was the very last thing she wanted to be doing this evening.

While she might be a gallery assistant by day, Merida was an actress by night—and also by heart. From England, she had come to New York with Broadway in mind and had given herself a year to make it.

Now, ten months in, her time and her savings were fast running out.

She needed money, and although she had an important audition tomorrow, and would prefer to be in her tiny apartment preparing for it, she smiled. 'It's honestly not a problem, Reece.'

'I had just started to lock up when Helene called.'

'Helene?'

'Ethan Devereux's PA. I can't *believe* that he's coming to visit the gallery and I shan't be here to show him around.'

'It will be fine.' Reece was highly strung and Merida did her best to calm him. 'What time is your flight?'

'At nine. If I'm going to make it then I have to leave soon.'

Reece made no move to go, though. Instead he fussed over details.

'You've read through the manual I sent you on the amulets?'

'Of course I have.' Merida nodded as she undid the belt of her trench coat. In fact, she had been the one who had set up the amulet display.

'This *has* to go well, Merida. I tried to suggest to Helene that he visit the gallery once I'm back from Egypt, but she was adamant that he wanted to see the display tonight. It would be madness to turn down a Devereux. One bad word from him and we're sunk.'

'Really?' Merida frowned. 'Just who is he?'

Reece let out a disbelieving laugh, but then righted himself. 'Of course—at times I forget you're from England and won't have grown up being fed every detail of the Devereux family's lives. Basically, the Devereux family are our landlords, darling.'

'They own the building?'

'They own half of the East Side and more besides. They're NYC royalty. There's the father—Jobe—and his two sons, Ethan and Abe. And all are utter bastards…'

'That's not nice.'

'*They're* not nice,' Reece countered. 'Oh, poor Elizabeth…'

'Who?'

'Elizabeth Devereux—Jobe's wife. Well, second wife, and mother to his sons. She was an absolute angel, and for a while they were almost a happy family.' Reece needlessly checked the door to make sure they were alone. 'Apparently she found out Jobe was having another affair.' He lowered his voice. 'Usually Elizabeth turned a blind eye, but rumour has it that this particular time it was with the nanny.'

'They broke up?'

'No, she fled to the Caribbean to heal, the poor thing, and died in a water-skiing accident. Since then the Devereux men have reeled from one scandal to the next. Don't let Ethan's unquestionable good looks dazzle you—he'd happily crush you in the palm of his hand.'

Merida winced.

'Now, there's champagne on ice. Pop the cork as soon as you see his car. I've had hors d'oeuvres from Barnaby's sent over…'

'How many guests is he bringing?' Merida checked.

'I'm not sure. Probably it's just his latest, so I've set up for two. I had a quick look online, to try and find out who she might be, but I got lost in the quagmire so you'll just have to wing it. Oh, and Gemma's brought you in one of her dresses to wear. It's out the back.'

'Pardon?' Merida's green eyes narrowed. She was unsure if she'd heard that right. Reece had never told her what to wear before.

'It's just a simple black dress. And Gemma's also loaned you some pearls.'

'What's wrong with what I'm wearing?'

Merida had on a gorgeous Buchanan tartan kilt. It was possibly a little short, but she had on black tights and suede boots and it was topped with a simple black jumper. It went well with her colouring and was her favourite outfit—one that she usually saved for auditions. But, given the important guest, she had made an extra effort this evening.

'You look fabulous,' Reece attempted. 'Merida, you always do. But while for the most part I'm happy to overlook your little eccentricities, with Ethan Devereux descending...'

'Eccentricities?' Merida frowned.

But Reece refused to be drawn and quickly changed the subject. 'Look, I really do appreciate this, Merida,' he said as he pulled up the handle on his suitcase. 'I'm sure there is some guy who hates me for calling you in to work tonight.'

Merida gave a non-committal smile. She had decided long ago that she would not be discussing her love-life with Reece. Or rather the absolute lack of it.

'And once Ethan's gone,' Reece said as he went

through the door, 'would you mind updating the website? Clint didn't get around to it.'

'Sure.'

Finally Reece was outside, chatting to Vince, the doorman-cum-security guard, as he hailed down a cab.

With fifteen minutes to prepare for the VIP guest's arrival, Merida slipped out to the back.

Unlike the gallery, which was all large open spaces, muted colours and plush fabrics, the back area was adorned with brown peeling paint and was terribly cramped.

There in the tiny staffroom, wrapped in plastic and hanging from the door, was a black dress, with a small pouch dangling from it, containing a single row of pearls.

Gemma had also left a pair of black stiletto shoes, and Merida's jaw gritted. They clearly didn't dare risk leaving even footwear to her! Reece could be so catty at times—but Merida needed the job far too much to protest.

She slipped the little black number on. It was a halter-neck, and Gemma hadn't taken into consideration the fact that Merida might not have a suitable bra. There was no choice but to go without—though thankfully Merida wasn't particularly well-endowed in that department.

Her make-up was the same as always—a touch of mascara to darken her fair lashes and bring out the green of her eyes, and a dash of blusher to brighten her pale skin. The only lipstick she had with her was a coral one, and she put a slick on, then stepped back and checked her reflection.

It looked rather dour—though there was far too much flesh on show to call it a funereal outfit, Merida thought. She looked like one of those greeters at an exclusive club or restaurant.

Except for the hair.

Merida would need a week to attain sleek sophistication in that department, so she ran some serum through the ends and then tied it so that it hung in a thick, low ponytail.

It would just have to do.

She headed out to the main gallery and cast a knowing eye over the displays, then clipped down the stairs to the amulets, just to check all was in order.

The lights were on a sensor, and the walls that led to the stunning exhibition were lined in very deep violet velvet. It gave the impression of entering another world.

Of course Reece would have ensured everything was immaculate for Mr Devereux, but she wanted to check for herself.

The amulets twinkled beguilingly. The next time she returned it would be with keys, so their guest could hold some of the choice pieces.

Happy that all was in order, Merida headed up to the main gallery and took her place on a high stool behind the desk. She tried to let go of the feeling of indignation Reece had left her with.

Eccentricities!

While acting might be her real passion, Merida worked hard at the gallery. Far harder than the manager, Clint, who thought only of commission and clearly hadn't been available this evening.

She was still smarting when an expensive black car pulled up outside. As the chauffeur got out she stepped down from the stool, popped the champagne and started to pour.

And then she glanced up.

A handmade leather shoe on the end of a suited leg was her first glimpse of him. Then he stepped out of the car and she saw his tall frame and immaculate suit. From his confident stance, Mr Devereux certainly *looked* as if he owned the street that he stood in.

She felt the coolness of champagne on her hand as the liquid fizzed over and stopped pouring. While she should have mopped up the mess, instead Merida chose to steal a moment and gaze upon his beauty while she had the chance.

Colour had not been on the artist's palette when *this* masterpiece had been created. His skin was pale, while his hair was as black as a raven's wing. As he turned his face and his eyes squinted in the late-afternoon sun she saw him in profile—and he was pure masculine elegance.

His absolute beauty flustered Merida.

Unusually so.

Stunning, elegant visitors regularly graced the gallery. At times the rich and famous did too.

He was more than that, though—only there wasn't

time to examine her thoughts…or rather the feelings this man stimulated in her.

With a hand-towel she blotted the tray and topped up the glass, and then poured another for any guest he might have brought. She looked outside, expecting a gorgeous beauty to have emerged from the car and flocked to his side.

But he walked towards the gallery alone.

Though she'd been warned about his good looks, nothing had prepared her for her reaction to them. Merida found that her lips were pressed together and her fingers dug into her palms. She unfurled them and smoothed the skirt of the dress, glad to have had a couple of minutes' warning of his magnificence in which to gather herself. But as the door opened and he stepped in, and she saw him without the barrier of glass, there came a knockout blow to her senses that had her internally reeling.

His eyes went straight to hers. They did not roam her body—he was too suave for that—and yet she felt a tingle on her skin as if they had.

'Mr Devereux…' Merida cleared her throat and drew on her acting skills as she grappled to find a more poised persona and fought not to blush as she extended her hand. 'It's lovely to meet you. I'm Merida Cartwright.'

'Merida.' His voice was rich and deep as he repeated her name and then said his. 'Ethan.' He invited her to use first-name terms as he briefly shook her hand.

Oh, his touch might have been fleeting, yet his

brief grip was firm, his skin warm enough to shoot out tiny volts. Like touching fire, the feeling intensified after contact, and Merida had to resist examining her fingers for a mark as she continued her introduction.

'I'm the gallery assistant…'

'Assistant?' Ethan checked abruptly, and the question in his tone told her that he had expected something better.

'Yes.' Merida swallowed. 'Reece would have loved to be here to take you around himself, but he's off to Egypt tonight.'

Ethan Devereux was less than impressed. Even at impossibly short notice he expected to be accommodated, and the fact that they had only managed to produce an assistant to show him around did not impress one bit.

Sheikh Prince Khalid of Al-Zahan—the owner of the amulets—was a personal friend and business colleague of Ethan's. They went way back, and had met years ago when studying at Columbia. Over dinner last night in Al-Zahan, Khalid had explained that he was worried that there were issues with the gallery to which he had loaned the royal collection. His sources stated that the staff were ill-informed, the tours somewhat rushed, and that patrons were steered towards the items that had the potential to earn most commission.

Khalid had asked Ethan to discreetly check things out.

Ethan had pointed out the fact that nothing he did

in New York City went unnoticed. But still, he had agreed to drop in at short notice and hopefully get a handle on what was going on. The fact that it was a mere assistant here to greet him scored the gallery its first black mark.

The fact that she was beautiful did not erase it.

'Before I take you through would you care for a drink…?' Merida offered.

'Let's just get started, shall we?'

He was brusque. Restless and impatient.

And he ignored the nibbles too.

Few did.

Merida had long since observed that at private viewings—even if guests staggered into the gallery after a three-course dinner—still most would sample the delicacies that had been laid on.

But Ethan Devereux didn't feel the need to partake in a free glass of champagne or caviar-laden blinis and succulent chocolate-dipped fruits.

He, Merida decided there and then, had no fear of missing out.

'Well, as I said, Reece is currently headed to Egypt. There he'll meet with Aziza…' Merida explained as they walked over to the first display. 'She's the designer of these exquisite dolls' houses.'

Shoot me now, Ethan thought.

Having found out that his father was unwell, and would tomorrow be undergoing surgery, Ethan had flown from Al-Zahan to Dubai and then home— albeit on his own luxury jet. Still, he did *not* want to be looking at dolls' houses—even if the walls *were* lined with hieroglyphics in gold.

Perhaps he should have some champagne—but that would only prolong things. He was running on empty and the jet-lag was really kicking in. He just wanted to cut the chatter and get to the amulets. But in order to glean as much as he could about the running of this gallery for Khalid he let her prattle on.

Well, not *prattle*, he conceded. Her voice was pleasant, in fact—prim and English—and her words were delivered with a throaty husk that made the topic *almost* bearable.

'These dolls' houses were kept for religious purposes,' Merida explained. 'They were never meant to be used as toys—certainly not for playing *mummies* and daddies.'

He didn't smile at her tiny well-worn joke, and even though he listened quietly she could tell that he was as bored as a three-year-old in church as they moved on.

They came to an exquisite silk rug—made, Merida explained, by Bedouin artisans using the vase weave technique.

'Ubaid, who oversees the making of every intricate piece, is a fierce protector of the craft.'

She started to explain about the natural dyes and the intricate patterns, and the endless hours that went in to creating such a masterpiece, but Ethan cut in.

'Next.'

Ethan *Philistine* Devereux, she silently named him. He certainly wasn't the first dismissive or bored client that Merida had taken through the gallery. Often people came to private viewings under silent sufferance—perhaps sent by their place of work or as a bored partner tagging along. And then there was the type who just *had* to have been and seen.

Yet he was alone—and it was he himself who had insisted on this viewing.

Merida ploughed on, but his impatience was palpable. So, as she showed him a jewellery exhibit, she toned down the details somewhat. Perhaps not enough, though, because as she showed him a ring Ethan yawned.

And not discreetly.

'Excuse me,' Ethan said.

He knew he was being rude, but he was genuinely exhausted. It certainly wasn't *her* fault that he had zero interest.

Or rather, zero interest in the displays.

The gallery assistant really was gorgeous.

Gorgeous.

There was an uptight quality to her that rather intrigued him, and something told him that despite her confident demeanour she was not quite as together as she seemed.

Her eyes were a deep mossy green, and as the tour progressed he noted how they repeatedly refused to hold his gaze.

She was slender, and her limbs were pale, with a dusting of pale freckles that had him wondering where the subtle golden trail led.

And as for that hair... It was like two of his favourite things—amber and cognac combined—and he tried to picture it free of its confines.

'And now to my favourite display.'

She smiled an enigmatic smile that made him wonder. Ethan could usually read women exceptionally well, and yet he could not quite read *her*.

'Which is…?' Ethan asked.

'The Amulets of Al-Zahan. We're extremely fortunate to have them on loan to us.'

'How long are they here for?'

'We've got them for three more months,' Merida said. 'Although we're hoping that can be extended. This way, please.'

Merida touched the switch that would turn on the lighting for the display and gestured with her head for him to head down the stairs.

'After you,' Ethan said.

For the first time—the *only* time—Merida wondered as to the merits of manners, for she found herself wishing that he had gone first.

The simple walk that she had made on so many occasions suddenly felt an impossible task. The velvet walls were too close, the lighting too dim, and she was utterly aware of him walking behind her.

The sensual darkness was for effect, of course. But it was having more of an effect on *her* than him.

Merida had undertaken the pinning of the velvet to the walls herself—the aim being to create a sort of portal…a sense of entering another time. However, she had never, as she'd stood on a stepladder and created this soft space, envisaged how it might feel to descend the stairs with a man like Ethan.

She trod more carefully than usual. She was nervous. Not so much aware that she might slip, more that if she did then it would be he who would steady her.

Merida had never reacted to anyone with such force. In fact she had never responded to a man in such a way.

She had wanted to. And she had tried on occasion—going along with a kiss while awaiting desire.

But it had never arrived and there had never been more than a kiss.

Merida had decided that her unwillingness must somehow be *her* fault—that there was something she was missing in her genes, or that her parents' bitter divorce and its aftermath had left her too mistrusting to let down her guard.

Oh, she could fake it for an audience. On stage, she could put on a sensual display indeed.

In fact, she was acting now—pretending that she had it all together and that he did not move her so.

Yet when the weekend came around, and she was back on stage where she felt she belonged, Merida knew she would draw on how it had felt to be so close to him.

In the real world, though, Merida was new to these feelings.

New to all this.

CHAPTER TWO

As MERIDA STEPPED out of the draped tunnel and into the semi-dark space, which twinkled with jewels, she found herself a little breathless.

There were no windows, no signs of the outside world to orientate oneself. The subtle bergamot and woody notes of Ethan Devereux's cologne were richer as she moved to where he stood, staring into the first display.

Merida cleared her throat and broke the heavy silence.

'These are the Amulets of Al-Zahan.'

Ethan had expected jewellery, or ancient carved tokens, but instead there was an array of gemstones, embedded in rocks, still in their original form. Each was a mini-galaxy in itself, and, far from being bored, he had rarely been so entranced as Merida started to tell their tale.

'The collection and its history was a passion of the late Queen Dalila of Al-Zahan. Right up to her death, some twenty years ago, she was still unearthing long-forgotten treasures.'

'How did she die?' Ethan asked.

'In childbirth. I believe it was her fourth child…' She faltered a little over a detail she did not know. 'I can check.'

'No need.'

Merida wasn't so sure. She felt as if she were being tested.

'On her marriage, she was given this amulet…'

In the first display cabinet was an intricate knot of emerald and ore. Beautifully lit, it turned slowly, and Ethan gazed upon it for a considerable time. The stone was practically bursting out of the ore.

'Amulets are a gift of potential,' Merida explained.

'Potential for what?'

'Marriages were, and still are, arranged in Al-Zahan. The amulets celebrate a future love, and also promote fertility. It is said that they are a gift of possibilities not yet fulfilled. To cut and polish the stone would reveal too many secrets.'

He seemed interested now, Merida thought as they moved on.

'The next amulet is Lapis Lazuli. Lapis was, and still is, ground to create a pigment for ultramarine— the colour used in Van Gogh's *Starry Night* painting. When the then Sheikha Princess was studying here in Manhattan she saw the painting on display. It is said it was the recollection of the painting that started her on a mission to find the missing amulets.'

'And did she find many?'

'Indeed.' Merida nodded. 'At the time of her death

she had made significant inroads—though of course there are many gaps.'

'And she studied here?' Ethan checked, more than interested now.

'Yes—at Columbia.'

It was the same college where Khalid and Ethan had met. He had known that the amulets belonged to Khalid's family, but he had not known that the late Queen had studied at Columbia too. It struck Ethan that he had learned more about the enigmatic Khalid from a stranger than from the man himself. He was more than intrigued as Merida spoke on.

'Princess Dalila returned to Al-Zahan to marry. However, her fondness for New York City was the reason that her son, Sheikh Khalid, agreed to the amulets being displayed here.'

Ethan moved on—but not out of boredom this time, more out of interest. He stood peering into the next display. Embedded within a large, egg-shaped piece of marble was a ruby.

'This one is my favourite,' Merida admitted.

She took out some black gloves and handed him a pair, then, as she put on her own gloves, Merida told him its story.

'Three hundred years ago in Al-Zahan there was a secret wedding,' she explained, and Ethan found he was drawing nearer to hear her low voice, as if she were sharing a secret only with him. 'Due to feuding between the two families there was no amulet given. Peace was finally restored, but after two years, when there were still no signs of a baby, it was decided that this was the reason. The Sheikh King, desperate for the lineage to continue, asked that the best stones be excavated. It took three years until what he considered a suitable offering was found.'

'It's stunning,' Ethan said, and so was the voice that told the tale.

She handed the large stone to him; he weighed it in his hand and then held it between finger and thumb, bringing it nearer to his eyes to examine it more closely.

'Careful,' Merida said, and drew on yet another of her well-worn lines. 'It ensures fertility.'

'For a hen, perhaps,' Ethan mused.

That tiny glint of humour made her smile. It reached her eyes, and they shone as beguiling as any amulet, and there was a single perfect moment when he forgot his hellish day.

Hellish because he should be in Dubai, finally kicking back, but instead would be heading to the hospital soon, where his father had been admitted in advance of some exploratory surgery that morning.

Ethan knew no more than that.

In an hour or so he would glean what he could, but for a moment or two he forgot the troubles awaiting him in the world outside. For now he focused on her smoky voice and the history of this beautiful stone, said to promote both love and fertility—two things he did not want.

'And did it work?' Ethan asked, handing the amulet back to her.

Merida nodded. 'Yes, the Sheikha Princess went on to have the first set of royal twins.'

The tour continued to its conclusion and, having seen and held some more amulets, Ethan handed the final piece to her and watched as she carefully replaced it in the display.

'The amulets really are beautiful—though it's all fairy tales of course.'

'I'm not so sure,' Merida said. 'All the marriages attached to these amulets were seemingly happy ones.'

'The Queen died in childbirth,' Ethan pointed out.

'They don't promise eternal life.' Merida smiled. 'I still think there's something rather magical about them.'

'Well, we'll have to agree to disagree on that point.'

Ethan didn't believe in love. Full stop.

But as for lust? Absolutely.

He was almost tempted to tell her now that he knew Khalid—that the Sheikh was, in fact, himself a twin. Though only to prolong the discussion. To talk with her some more.

'How long have you worked at the gallery?' he asked as they headed back up the stairs.

'Almost a year.'

Merida certainly wasn't going to admit that she had been hauled in this afternoon at the last moment, but as they came out from the tunnel she did admit that this wasn't her full-time job.

'Though I only work here part-time.'

'More of a hobby, then?' he asked, or rather assumed, for he was more than used to women whose daddies found them a 'little job' until a suitable husband came along.

'Not quite,' Merida said, and gave him a tight smile without elaborating further.

Ethan Devereux was here to see the gallery, not hear her life story.

They walked past the displays where he had stood bored, and then came back to the desk. Of course she offered him a drink once more, and waved a hand over the nibbles.

Again, he declined.

'Do you have any more questions?' Merida asked, just as she always did, and yet it felt a little different this time. The beguiling, sensual air surrounding the amulet display seemed still to cling, and she found that she held her breath as she awaited his response.

'Just one...' Ethan said.

He saw her blink rapidly, and rather thought that she'd guessed what his question was.

Dinner.

And it should be as seamless as that—because for Ethan it always was.

Yet he hesitated, and did not know why.

It wasn't the fact that he had to head to the hospital that halted him from asking. He could offer to pick her up in an hour.

Yet he didn't.

Instead he reminded himself he was here for Khalid.

'The rugs,' he said. 'If I were to order one, how long would it take to make?'

'It would depend on the size.'

'One like that.'

Merida should be dancing on the spot at the unexpected chance of earning some commission. A commissioned rug was worth a fortune, and she should be engaging him and wowing him with details. Yet all she could think of was dinner. Or rather, the lack of it.

Which was just as well, given Reece's warning that he would crush her in the palm of his hand.

Yet Merida suddenly wanted to experience the feel of his palm more than she had wanted anything before in her life.

Except Broadway, which she had dreamed of all her life.

Ethan Devereux, whom she had only just met, suddenly came a very close second.

Merida stood there, trying to unscramble her mind so she could answer his question as to how long a commissioned rug would take to make.

'I would think around eighteen months.'

'What if I wanted it sooner?'

'Ubaid has many artisans. If they were focused on one piece, perhaps a year…'

'And what if I wanted it sooner than that?' he pushed.

'I'm afraid it would take time. Patience.'

Reece might never forgive her, but instead of promising limitless artisans, all devoted to pleasing this man who could name his price, she told him instead that he would have to wait.

Only they weren't talking about rugs. She was quite sure of that.

And so was he.

'I don't have patience,' Ethan said, and the words were delivered with a slight snap, for he knew now why he hadn't invited her to dinner.

For it would be *just* dinner.

And then another dinner.

No, he did not have the patience for that.

He wanted to know how she tasted rather than where she was from and what she was like.

And so, instead of pushing, he ended the encounter.

'Well,' he said, 'thank you for the tour. It's been interesting.'

Unexpectedly so. And in unexpected ways, he thought.

Merida saw him to the door and then stood, her smile fixed, as they shook hands again, but for a dangerous second longer than the first time.

She did not glance down at his hands but she could feel each of his fingers, long and slender, as they closed around hers. And she breathed through her mouth, rather than her nose, for the scent of him had her wanting to draw closer.

'It was a pleasure to meet you,' Merida said through lips that did not want to talk. It was as if they yearned to meet his.

She wanted to return to the dark velvet space from which they had so recently emerged.

What the hell was happening to her?

'Thank you for visiting,' Merida said calmly, when *Get out, get out, get out* was what she wanted to scream. Only her acting experience allowed composure to reign on her features.

He didn't say thank you again.

And he didn't wish her a good evening.

Ethan Devereux simply left.

And he left behind a vortex within her.

She watched the doorman farewell him, and the driver open his car door, and as he disappeared inside Merida learned that she could breathe again.

The devil had left the building.

CHAPTER THREE

HIS DRIVER TOOK him the short distance to the hospital, and to a rear entrance so that he would not be seen arriving.

This must not get out.

Tomorrow morning Jobe Devereux was having a minor planned procedure, but that very knowledge would be enough to spook their shareholders.

Ethan was concerned enough to have flown home.

His PA, Helene, had given him directions and Ethan took the elevator up to the private wing.

His father might as well be in his office, Ethan thought as he knocked on his door and walked in.

Abe was there, and so too was Maurice, their head of PR.

'Ethan!' His father, sitting in a leather chair, looked surprised to see him. 'What can I do for you?'

Do for him?

There was no real welcome, and no invitation to take a seat. Their relationship had long been a strained one—perhaps because they were incredibly alike, and not just in looks.

The Devereux men were all private, but they all had an intrinsic licentious edge.

His father, though, had done nothing in his life to curb it.

'I came to see you.' Ethan did his best to keep his voice even. 'And to see if there was anything I could do to help.'

'Oh, it's no big deal,' Jobe said. 'I'll be back in the office on Monday.'

'How was Dubai?' Abe asked as he closed his laptop, clearly just about to leave. 'Did you look at the hotel site?'

'I did.' Ethan nodded. 'But I was thinking…' He paused. Ethan was rather more interested in the potential of Al-Zahan, but decided now wasn't the time to talk about it. 'Helene's writing up the report.'

'Good,' Abe said. 'Maurice and I are going to get dinner—are you coming?'

Ethan shook his head. 'I've already eaten.'

He hadn't actually eaten since the plane, and that had been several hours ago, but Ethan simply wasn't in the mood for more business talk, and with Maurice and Abe that was all it would be.

Once he was alone with his father it was somewhat awkward.

While it might look like a plush office or a hotel room, Ethan could now see the room held subtly placed equipment, and the antiseptic in the air gave it a slight nauseating edge.

'Where's Chantelle?'

Ethan didn't generally enquire about the whereabouts of his father's latest lover, but five minutes into his visit the conversation had already run out.

'We broke up.'

'When?'

'Do I ask *you* about *your* love life?' Jobe barked.

'No, but only because I don't have one,' Ethan said.

He had a *sex* life, and fully intended to keep it at that. He'd seen the damage relationships caused. His father's marital history was on par with Henry VIII's. Well, minus the beheadings and with the added fact that not one of Jobe's marriages had survived.

But there had been plenty of divorces.

And his mother had died.

Ethan could not forgive his father for that.

Not her death. More the circumstances.

Ethan had been five when she'd died, but he had been ten, maybe eleven, when he'd finally decided to find out for himself if the rumours about his father having an affair with their nanny were true.

Sure enough, the papers at the time had spoken of a huge argument, and Elizabeth Devereux leaving home sobbing and heading for JFK.

He'd looked at endless photos of the happy family they had once been and had confronted his father.

'You had everything and you ruined it. Is that why Meghan left?' he'd asked.

Jobe had sat silently nursing a drink as his youngest son had raged. Only as he'd stormed off had he called out.

'Ethan! Get back here!'

'Go to hell!' He had run upstairs, taking down one of family pictures that hung on the wall and throwing it at him. 'I hate you for what you did.'

It had never been spoken of again. The picture had been rehung, and to this day remained in its place on the wall, and still they avoided any topics of the personal kind.

But now, given his father was having surgery, Ethan tried.

'So, what's happening tomorrow?'

Ethan wanted specifics. But Jobe refused to give them.

'It's just a minor procedure.' His father shrugged. 'Exploratory.'

'Can't they just do a scan or something?'

'Oh, so you went to med school now?'

'I'm just saying I don't understand what you're going to theatre for.'

'That's what we're finding out.'

They went in ever-widening circles, talking about everything and nothing and getting nowhere fast.

'I'm going down at eight in the morning and I'll be back up here by nine. I wanted to stay home the night before the op, but Prof Jacobs insisted I came in.'

'Because had you been at home you would have ignored his instructions to have only a light supper and forgo your nightcap,' Ethan said.

'True,' Jobe admitted. 'Look, if you really want to do something for me then you can attend the Carmody function.'

If Ethan hadn't known already that something

was seriously wrong with his father, he knew it then. The Carmody function had been an annual feature on his father's calendar for as long as Ethan could recall. Amongst the many pictures on the walls of his father's home was one of his parents standing on the red carpet there.

The ball was more than two weeks away. For his father to be pulling out now sent a shiver of dread down Ethan's spine. Not that he showed it. Instead, he agreed to attend in his father's place.

'You'll need a date to take with you,' Jobe huffed.

'I'm sure that can be arranged.' There was nothing left to say. 'I'll come and see you in the morning.'

'No, don't,' Jobe warned. 'The damn press is on to me. I'm sure of it.'

'On to what?' Ethan challenged.

For a moment near identical black eyes met, but Jobe wasn't about to open up to anyone.

'Just carry on as normal. The professor will let one of you boys know when I'm back from the OR.'

Boys.

His father still referred to him and Abe as boys, when they were thirty and thirty-four respectively, but there was no affection in the term. If anything, it was said dismissively.

With the duty visit done, Ethan walked through the private wing and towards the elevator, turning right with little thought even though he'd never been there before.

Then he halted.

Ethan *had* been there before.

Shards of memory felt as if they were working their way to the surface of his brain as he stood waiting for the elevator. He looked down the corridor and could almost see himself—five years old and dressed in his new school uniform, accompanied by his new nanny and walking beside Abe as they headed out from a waiting room to go and visit their mother.

To say goodbye.

He took the elevator, trying to banish the memory, yet as he stepped out into the brightly lit foyer he recalled it again. The press had been waiting outside, but their instructions that day had been different from usual—*Don't wave or smile. Look sad.*

Who had told a couple of kids that? Ethan thought as he walked quickly to the waiting car. Who the hell had told them how to act, how to *react*, on the day their mother died?

His long stride halted as the answer came to him—the new nanny had.

His driver was waiting, but Ethan dismissed him. He wanted to walk—to get rid of the hospital scent which still filled his nostrils.

Suddenly, twenty-five years on, he was back to that day and the utter bewilderment he'd felt.

The grief.

And the guilt—oh, yes, the guilt.

Because he hadn't missed his mother as everyone had assumed he must.

Meghan.

It was his nanny, Meghan, he had missed at that time.

* * *

The gallery website was a constant thorn in Merida's side.

Clint had been supposed to update it before he'd headed off to an art fair, though of course he hadn't.

And with Reece being away Merida needed to change the opening times advertised there. Especially as she wouldn't be here tomorrow morning because of her audition.

It was for a prime-time television show and, while excited, Merida was incredibly nervous about it. She *had* to get the part. Although theatre was her passion, Merida desperately needed credits to her name—and as well as that she *loved* the show. It would be a huge boost for her résumé as well, and who knew what doors it might open?

So she updated the opening and closing times on the website, and a few other things, and then, instead of clicking off and closing down the computer, Merida couldn't resist looking Ethan up.

God, he was beautiful.

His dark, slightly hooded eyes were so *brooding*, and in every photo she saw, that mouth utterly refused to smile.

Just as it had refused to smile with her.

For a moment she let herself wonder how it might feel to be in the path of his gentler gaze.

Merida drank the glass of champagne that Ethan hadn't wanted and nibbled on the caviar blinis he'd declined as she gazed upon his image.

Then she ate dark-chocolate-covered blueberries and read about the man who quite simply intrigued her.

Reece had been right. His life was a quagmire indeed—and Ethan Devereux's playboy status was well-documented. His older brother Abe's was too, although he seemed to have settled down a touch of late. As for his father...

Goodness!

It would seem that all the Devereux men dated and discarded with ease. It was Ethan she wanted to find out more about. Yet they all seemed inextricably linked.

Merida clicked on a recent news article: *Twenty-Five Years On.*

There was a photo of the Devereux men in dark suits and ties at what appeared to be a memorial service. Merida read that a quarter-century ago his mother had been involved in an accident in the Caribbean. She had been flown back to New York, but had died two days later.

The country had mourned—particularly here in New York City—and there had been accusations against her husband.

Merida topped up her glass as she read about the rumours that Jobe Devereux had been embroiled in a salacious affair, rumoured to be with the nanny, and that that was the reason poor Elizabeth had fled.

Merida raised her eyebrows.

Certainly if she found out *her* husband was sleeping with the nanny she'd be kicking him out, rather than running off.

Still, it made good reading.

There were photos of the two Devereux children, accompanied by nannies, arriving at the hospital to say goodbye.

How awful, Merida thought, but how riveting!

So engrossed was she that she barely looked up when the gallery door opened.

'We're actually closed,' Merida said—and then promptly wanted to die when she turned. Because there were few things more embarrassing than looking up to see the object of your desire at the very same time you were looking him up online.

He now had on a long dark coat, worn open over his suit. There was an emergency button under the desk and Merida was rather tempted to push it. Not because she felt threatened—not in the least. Just because every cell in her body had moved to high alert.

'Hi,' Merida said, and probably undid all the changes she had made to the website as she frantically clicked the mouse in an attempt to delete him from the screen. 'Did you forget something?'

'You know I did.'

Merida swallowed, and though she could have cast her eyes around for his keys, or a forgotten tablet, or anything else that might have forced his return, deep down she knew what he was about to ask.

And he didn't disappoint. 'How about dinner?'

There were many reasons that she should say no to his offer. Merida had been warned about his reputation—not just by his terrible press, but also by Reece. And possibly the hairs that stood up on her bare arms should have served as another reason to decline.

Yet that shiver was borne of awareness rather than nervousness, Merida was certain.

He made her *aware* of her own body.

Ethan Devereux reminded her, without a word or even a gaze in that direction, that she was not wearing a bra, because suddenly her small breasts felt tight and heavy, and her legs, even though she was sitting, felt weak.

He made her want to throw caution to the wind and say yes.

'I have to close up first.'

'Of course.'

Her legs felt as if they might give way as she stepped down from the stool.

Everything that she usually did so easily suddenly felt new and unfamiliar.

From walking to breathing, she had to focus anew over and over again.

She tidied up the gallery as he wandered around, looking again at the exhibitions.

'I'll go and get changed,' Merida said, but he gave a brief shake of his head.

'No need.'

In the tiny staffroom Merida wondered if Gemma would mind if the little black dress and pearls were taken out for the night. Surely any woman would understand?

Merida re-tied her hair and then topped up her lipstick. She placed her kilt, jumper and boots in her bag and slipped on her trench coat. When she came out of the staffroom he had given up on the exhibits and was scrolling through his phone.

She did her usual walk-around, and Ethan said he'd wait outside as she finished up.

In fact, aware that she was somewhat distracted by the six feet two of testosterone waiting for her, Merida took extra care, turning off the computer and lights and then setting the alarm and locking up with diligence.

When the gallery was secured, she stepped onto the chilly street and turned—and there he was.

Merida wished there was a code that might secure her heart.

She stood watching the most beautiful man on the most beautiful street lounging against the wall, and then he turned to walk towards her, his long coat flapping behind him in the breeze.

'There's something else that I forgot,' Ethan said.

'Oh?'

She cast her mind again to keys and laptops, whatever it was that she might have locked up in the gallery, and it took a second for her to register to what he was referring.

It wasn't just asking her to dinner that he'd forgotten. Ethan had omitted a kiss.

On a night that was turning a bit chilly, and under a sky that was being painted a dusky rose, the setting was photo-perfect.

Merida wanted to capture the dusk of the park, the yellow of the taxis—how the world appeared in the seconds before he kissed her. She would be kissed here, Merida realised, and this moment would be seared in her memory for life.

He cupped her face in her hands and she stared deep into his eyes. While there was not a fleck of colour that she could perceive in his gaze, there was depth and complexity and hues from another realm.

He was perfect.

And so was his kiss.

His lips were firm, yet with traces of tenderness. She wanted to keep her eyes open, just to capture each second, yet there was no chance of that, for his kiss was so exquisite that her eyes closed, so that she could fully sink into its measured bliss.

He pulled her closer, and she was wrapped in the warmth of his arms as the cool spring air between them evaporated. His tongue was warm, and tasted like a cocktail designed solely for her. She felt dizzy, yet steady in the capture of his embrace, and when he kissed her harder the roughness of his jaw and the smoky notes of his cologne inflamed her.

She kissed him back with an ardour that had been missing in every other kiss and in her every imagining to date.

And then—cruelly, but necessarily—before they edged towards the indecent, he tore his mouth away.

He had *started* their date with a kiss.

CHAPTER FOUR

'GOOD EVENING, MR DEVEREUX,' the doorman greeted him. 'Madam.'

They walked through the sumptuous foyer of a luxurious hotel that was filled with columns of flowers and beautiful people milling about.

He was greeted everywhere by name, and clearly *that* name did not require a prior booking.

Merida was relieved of her coat and bag at the restaurant, and the maître d' led them to a table, beautifully set for two.

The restaurant was stunning, with an old-fashioned New York elegance, subtle music and a dance floor. Beside the windows there were candelabras, taller than Ethan, and even with the huge chandelier that sparkled above the dance floor the lighting was subdued enough that there was a shroud of intimacy as they took their seats.

Merida was nervous. Far more nervous than she dared to let on. So she breathed her way through their seating, and then the pouring of champagne, and pretended she was seated at a table onstage, because it was easier than the reality of sitting opposite him.

The first thing he did was switch off his phone, and that small gesture told her they would not be interrupted.

'Well, here we are,' Ethan said and they clinked glasses. 'It's good to be back.'

'Back?' Merida checked. 'D'you come here a lot, then?'

'I meant back in New York. I've been away for a few weeks.'

'On holiday?' Merida asked, but he gave a small shake of his head.

'Work,' Ethan said. It always was.

The food was delectable, but it wasn't the hors d'oeuvres Merida had consumed that killed her appetite, it was the overwhelming presence of *him*. He didn't put her at instant ease; instead he kept her on a delicious edge.

Merida chose a burnt butter and sage ravioli, and Ethan ordered steak. She noted that the waiter didn't ask how he would like it done. He already knew.

It was the tiniest detail, yet it served as a reminder for Merida that this was not new to him as it was to her.

'So you've been at the gallery for nearly a year?' Ethan prompted, as if their earlier conversation was still left unfinished.

'For ten months,' Merida said. 'As I said, I'm just there part-time. I'm actually an actress.'

Ethan looked over, his dark eyes narrowing a fraction. He had dated more than a few actresses in his time, and was generally suspicious of them. Most wanted to hook their rising star into his or milk their fifteen minutes of fame when things ended between them.

As they inevitably did.

'It's all I've ever wanted to be,' Merida admitted. 'I wasn't getting very far back home, so I decided to try my luck here.'

'Home being England?' he checked.

'Yes.' Merida nodded. 'London. Although, as my father pointed out, if I can't get work in London then why should New York be any different?'

Ethan raised an eyebrow. Her father didn't sound particularly encouraging, but he made no comment, just listened.

'Still, it's the dream. Right now I've got a small part in an even smaller production.'

'What's it called?'

'Near Miss.'

He gave a shake of his head, to indicate that he'd never heard of it. 'And what part do you play?'

'Arrow,' Merida said, and then clarified a touch. 'I'm an arrow. And I keep missing my mark.'

'Are you *dressed* as an arrow?'

'No. I'm dressed from head to toe in black. I wear a black leotard and tights and a long black wig.'

He looked at her lovely red hair and, although he knew little about acting or costumes, he was an expert at opinions. 'I think they might have missed an opportunity there.'

'Meaning?'

'I'd have thought that a red-headed arrow would be more telling.'

'The lead wears a red wig.' Merida smiled. 'The arrow is more like her shadow self. A smaller part.'

'But a *very* important one,' Ethan said. 'Though of course I may be somewhat biased.'

Merida's hand shook a little as she took a sip of water. He was so subtle, so *sparing* with his words, that his suggestion of bias towards her had come from left field.

Ethan made her his sole focus, and that was rare. He made it clear there was nowhere else he wanted to be, Merida thought as their meals arrived. There was no feeling that he would soon have to dash, as her parents often did when she called. Reece too, come to that. And there was no looking over his shoulder to check who might appear, as so many in the acting world did.

'Do you miss your family?'

'Sometimes.' Merida nodded again. 'My parents are divorced, and both have remarried…' Her voice trailed off and she didn't elaborate.

Ethan wanted her to. It was rare that he wanted to know more about any woman he would soon bed.

And bed her he would.

That decision had been made when he had dismissed his driver and walked back towards the gallery.

At first he had thought he had left it too late, as the gallery had appeared closed, but on looking in he had seen her sitting at the high desk.

She was beautiful.

Nothing like the coiffed, sophisticated beauties he usually dated. Her riot of hair and that full mouth entranced him almost as much as those bewitching green eyes. Yes, he wanted to know more about her—but it was not just for that reason alone he decided to share a part of himself.

He wanted to talk.

Tonight he would kill for normality, to be able to admit to another person from where he had just come. To speak, as anyone else would, when they were worried about a family member.

But that type of conversation was off-limits when you were a Devereux.

And so he spoke of the past—of things that were more freely known.

'I know all about divorce,' he said. 'My father's been married a few times. Once before my mother died and twice since.'

'Do you ever see your stepmothers?'

'God, no,' Ethan said, and gave a little shudder at the thought. 'All those marriages, apart from my parents', were pretty short-lived.'

'So you didn't get close to any of them?'

'Not at all.' Ethan shook his head and gave a small mirthless laugh. 'I don't think they were ever love-matches. It was more financial bliss those women were seeking. Mind you, I can hardly blame them.

My father just wanted a wife on his arm for functions. He was never home.'

'Who brought you up, then?'

'Draconian nannies,' Ethan said, and then he halted, realising he had said far more than he usually would. He turned the conversation back to Merida. 'How old were you when your parents divorced?'

'I was ten when they broke up, and they spent the next two years fighting over shared access of me.'

'You were popular, then?' He gave a light tease, but she didn't smile.

'I don't think either of them actually *wanted* shared care—they just didn't want to give in to the other.'

There was still hurt there when she thought back to that time. Although she felt silly sometimes, when she heard what others had gone through—like Ethan, who had not only lost his mother but then had to endure an endless parade of stepmothers.

He watched her fall silent and put down her cutlery. She stared at it for a moment, silently, but when the waiter came and asked if everything was okay she turned and gave a bright smile.

'Amazing, thank you.'

The mask was back.

Ethan read women very easily. In fact, he read most people with ease.

He just couldn't quite read Merida.

She was friendly, and appeared confident, yet there was a vulnerability to her that he could not place. It was more that he sensed it rather than saw it.

'Did either of your parents have more children?' Ethan asked.

'Yes.' Merida's smile remained. 'My father had a son and my mother a daughter.'

'Are you close to them?'

'I see them when I can, and I babysit,' she said, not really answering the question.

'Babysit?' He frowned. 'How old are the children?'

'Oh, they're ten and eleven now. I mean, I used to take them to their sports clubs and such, when I was able. You know…if their parents couldn't manage it.'

'I expect it's been nice having a break, then.'

'I don't mind doing it—when I can, of course. I don't want them to miss out on stuff.'

'Such as…?''

'Activities.'

'Did you?'

Oh, please don't ask me this, Merida thought.

She did not want to go there and ruin a perfectly lovely night, but it felt as if he'd suddenly skipped the niceties and gone straight to the jugular.

It was just a question, she told herself.

But a pertinent one.

'It's really not that big a deal,' Merida said.

'Then you won't mind sharing.'

'Of course not. I got cast in a big West End theatre production,' Merida finally said. 'When I was twelve. It was huge. Of course they were very strict about performing hours for children, and really you needed to have your parents completely on board. At first they were really encouraging,' Merida said, and then an edge came into her voice. 'I'm certain that was more for the courts, though.'

Oh, she *did* mind sharing this, and fought to find a more relaxed tone.

'The rehearsals were for six weeks, and at first either my mum or dad was always there to pick me up. But then it got more difficult. Dad had a new job, and my mum and I moved quite a distance away...'

'You had to let it go?'

Merida nodded. She didn't go into detail—how much it had hurt to let go of the part she had coveted and worked so hard for. How lost and confused she had felt when, once joint custody had finally been awarded, when the war was over in a tie, Merida hadn't felt particularly wanted by either of her parents.

That would be a bit much for a first date.

And then she qualified that thought, not really sure if this could be classified as a date.

As the waiter cleared their plates all Merida knew was that here was where she wanted to be—even if she found him daunting. Only it wasn't his wealth or his financial prowess that daunted her, and it wasn't even his reputation with women.

It was this.

How much she liked him.

His utter ability to make the world disappear.

They could be sitting in a late-night diner eating burgers and she would feel exactly as she did now—*connected*.

She was telling Ethan things she had only ever told her closest friend, Naomi.

'How much longer are you in New York?' Ethan asked.

'That depends,' Merida said, and then admitted the truth. 'I'm nearing desperation if I want to stay here.'

She didn't want to bring the night down with cold facts. But, as much as she loved performing in *Near Miss*, it paid just a tiny stipend, and her work at the gallery covered little more than the rent.

Although there *was* still hope.

'I've got an audition tomorrow morning, for a part on a prime-time television show.'

'What part?'

'You won't laugh?'

'I rarely do.'

'A hooker,' Merida said. 'And a corpse. Although you might not believe it, playing a corpse *does* involve acting.'

He didn't laugh, but he *did* smile.

And when he did, while looking in her eyes, even as she went to return it Merida faltered, because it made her toes curl beneath the table. How, she wondered, could he move her so with just a slight shift in that sulky mouth? It was as if he'd reached inside her and effortlessly turned up an inner flame.

And she smiled back.

Her first real smile of the night.

Her façade fell away and they sat, staring at each other. She felt so *right*, so *recognised*, that when his hand reached across the table she did not jump. Instead her hand closed around his in relief.

She felt *found*.

The waiter returned and it felt like an intrusion for both of them as they dropped contact and took the dessert menus.

The words blurred, and the whimsical descriptions were lost on Merida as she accepted they were headed for bed.

Oh, yes. She had waited a long time to feel like this.

And now, as she tried to read about meringues and mousses and all things delicious, she attempted to fathom his reaction if she told him of her untouched status.

'What would you like?' Ethan asked.

Colour that she could not tame flooded her cheeks and chest.

'I'm not sure that I want anything,' Merida admitted.

'Well, I do,' Ethan said, and put down the menu. He stood. 'I want to dance.'

He led her to the dance floor, and once there it was a relief for her to be back in his arms.

Not so much a relief, because his touch so readily inflamed her, but it was bliss to be held by him.

So skilfully held.

They might have danced this dance a hundred times, Merida thought, for he held her as if he had practised over and over doing just that.

It was as if Ethan's arms *knew* her.

His hand was above the small of her back and the pressure was light, yet still firm. He pulled her in closer and she wrapped her arm around his, so her hand came to rest beneath his shoulder blade and she could put her head high on his chest.

If it all ended now it would still be the best night of her life.

Except she didn't want it to end now.

He had pulled her in a fraction closer, and his hand had moved up enough that his palm grazed the naked skin of her upper back. Then the pads of his fingers dusted the notches of her spine and she closed her eyes at the sensual bliss and wondered how it would go from here.

Would he kiss her again and suggest they get a room? Or would her drive her home and expect an invitation to come in?

She had no idea how this worked.

He was so sophisticated, so utterly at ease with all this, and from her response to his touch no doubt he thought the same of her.

Did she *have* to tell him she was a virgin? Merida pondered. She'd acted the part of a lover on stage—could she take that into real life?

She knew now. Merida knew why she was still a virgin—for no one had made her feel like he did. Quite simply, he made the rest look like rank amateurs.

'Merida,' he said, in a low growly voice, and she lifted her face to hear what he had to say. 'Come to bed.'

He could see the heat spread on her cheeks and the rapid blink shuttering her glittering eyes, but he did not retract or soften his invite. Ethan wanted her very much. He had chosen to walk here from the hospital for the chance of seeing her again.

For this.

'Ethan…'

He saw the slight conflict in her eyes and felt the sudden tension in her, and then she spoke again.

'I haven't done this before.'

She really *was* difficult to read, for he'd misread her now.

Not for a second had he considered that the sensual dancer in his arms, who had kissed him back so sexily and deeply on the street, was a virgin.

But Ethan was more than used to this kind of guilty declaration before a one-night stand—the insistence that this wasn't usually the case before a woman came tumbling into his bed.

So he went along with it.

'Who knew we'd both get so carried away?' he said.

He kissed her then—right there on the dance floor.

Not a kiss to her mouth, but he lowered his head and dropped a slow kiss on her bare shoulder, and the heat from his mouth made her stomach fold over on itself.

And then he came back to her face, his mouth by her ear, and his words and the breath with which they were delivered caused her neck to arch.

'Come to bed, Merida.'

Yes.

CHAPTER FIVE

HIS HAND WAS tight around hers as they stepped into an elevator and Merida glimpsed herself in the mirrored walls. But it was Ethan's reflection that she cared to see, and apart from the dark shadow on his jaw he looked so polished and poised that he might be on his way to meeting, rather than taking her to bed.

She was the giveaway.

Her eyes were huge in her face, Merida saw, and it was only the grip of his hand that tethered her to his side, because she simply wanted to wrap herself around him.

Of course here was not the place.

Another couple came in and Ethan stepped back a little to make space for them, prompting Merida to do the same.

Her mind was on things other than normal social niceties.

How, she wondered, did his seamless world work?

Had he booked a suite prior to their arrival?

She didn't know. And, as his thumb pressed into the palm of her hand, she didn't much care.

The other couple got out, and Merida noted that the woman turned and stole another glance at Ethan. She heard them speaking as the doors slid closed.

'I'm sure that was Abe Dev—'

Ethan didn't comment. No doubt he was used to being recognised, or mistaken for his brother, wherever he went. And although they might have the wrong brother, for Merida he was *right*.

So very, *very* right.

Merida did not know what floor they were on.

And she did not know where the corridor they'd stepped into led.

They just walked along plush cream carpets until he swiped a lock, and Merida knew that her long-awaited dreams lay behind this door.

The suite was beyond her imaginings.

It was elegantly furnished, with soaring ceilings, and though the heavy silk drapes were closed on the New York skyline the view was still spectacular—for it was of *him*.

Merida cared little for her surroundings.

Ethan Devereux had mesmerised her from the very moment he had appeared in her life. It seemed impossible that it had been just hours ago they had met, and that as recently as this afternoon she hadn't even known of his existence.

He took off his jacket and tossed it onto a chair.

Through a large half-open door she could see a vast four-poster bed, draped in cream silk with the sheets turned back. Merida felt a combination of excitement and terror as she wondered at his reaction if he found out this was her first time.

She decided that he must not.

Ethan poured two drinks from a heavy brandy decanter. He brought one over to her and Merida took a sip, willing her nerves to calm. The cognac was warm, and it burnt a little as it went down.

Though she didn't suffer with stage fright, she felt as if she had it tonight. Not that she showed it. For when she felt Ethan staring she gave him a sensual smile that beckoned, and he walked over and took her face in his hands.

His touch was warm, and his kiss this time was thorough, and when his tongue slipped inside her mouth he tasted of the cognac she had just sipped, and of sin, and of all that had been missing until now.

His hands roamed her body, feeling first the smoothness of her back and then making a more intimate perusal of her spine, from the naked tip at the nape of her neck down to the base, where his mere touch had her hips melding into him.

His hand moved between them and stroked the underside of her breast, and then his thumb grazed her nipple. She moaned into his mouth, because the contact was heady bliss and yet not enough.

His other hand worked the knot of her halter-neck dress. He paused their kiss so that he could peel the fabric down until, save the pearls, she was naked from the waist up.

His eyes lingered on her breasts, and in response to his gaze they peaked. And then his warm fingers met the naked flesh. He toyed with them both and she began to shake—an involuntary tremble as nerves and anticipation combined to make her unsteady.

She should *do* something, Merida thought, going back to her trick of pretending to be someone she was not.

So she reached for his tie, unknotting it as he played with her breasts, seductively gazing at his mouth as she slid the tie off.

Her fingers grew impatient as she dealt with the buttons on his shirt, but as she parted the fabric her reward was there. There was a dark smattering of hair over a wide chest, and flat nipples the deep red of his mouth. She pushed his shirt down over his shoulders and let the palms of her hands explore his torso.

He was toned and magnificent. She could feel the muscle and sinew and imagined being wrapped tightly in his arms. Then her hands slid down and her fingers toyed with the snake of black hair on his flat stomach.

She could see the thick bulge beneath, and she could feel him too. She was nervous and trying not to show it as she imagined that long, thick length inside her.

'Take it out,' he commanded roughly.

Merida was hesitant, her fingers shaking as she unzipped him. When she had freed him he sprang free, and she held him warm, strong and alive in her hand. She felt her lips press together, nervous and unsure of herself.

He closed her hand with his, tight around his solid length, and she watched, mesmerised, as together they stroked, feeling the power they generated building with each movement.

He released her then, and impatiently backed her against the wall with firm kisses, his hands pulling down her dress. As she stepped out of it she looked up to see him sheathing himself.

Her knickers were the only barrier left, and now he was back to kissing her hard, tearing the silk with his big hands. She had never known such male power.

'Ethan...'

His face was rough on hers and he felt delicious, but she knew she could not let it go unsaid.

'I'm a virgin.'

He halted, wondering if he'd misheard, or if it was a game.

And then he looked into her eyes, glittering with both lust and terror, and understood what Merida had meant when she'd said she'd never done this before.

He should halt proceedings—he knew that. In fact, he tore off the condom. But then he saw her unshed tears, and the battering of old memories, his fears for his father, were all swept aside by her gaze.

'Do you want to be here?' Ethan asked her.

'Yes!' Merida almost wept, and then she attempted the impossible: an assured smile.

She moved in to resume kissing him, but Ethan

pulled his face back. 'Then stop pretending,' he said, for he knew now that her confidence was a lie.

'I don't know how to!'

It was the most honest admission of her life.

She did not know how. How to stop smiling and saying things were fine when they weren't.

She did not know how to voice her needs.

Acting was easy, for she was playing a part and being told how to be. In the real world she simply did not know.

He kissed her, hard and rough, and she felt the bruise of his lips when she wanted tenderness, the scratch of his jaw as she matched his fervour.

Again he hauled himself back. 'I told you to stop pretending. Stop trying to please me.'

She felt as if she might cry, for it was as if he had discovered her naked beneath a lifetime of disguises.

And then he spoke. 'You're doing it anyway.'

It was the nicest thing he could have said, and when a tear fell he dusted the apple of her cheek with his mouth until her lips parted of their own accord and tears rolled down.

Each kiss, no matter how softly delivered, felt like a chisel, tapping away and exposing the real Merida beneath.

He tasted the salt of her tears and carried her to the bed. He stood over her and took off the pearls, her shoes, and even her hair tie until she was utterly naked.

The condom had gone, and his jacket was back

in the lounge. At the sight of her triangle of copper curls he mentally cursed, for there were some moments that should go uninterrupted.

For the first and only time that night she sensed his distraction as his eyes darted from where she lay on the bed to the door.

And then she understood. 'I'm on the Pill.'

'Never, *ever* say those words to a bastard like me.'

'Not even one that I'm crazy about?'

A flag should have been raised. He was being warned that she was in too deep. But he ignored it.

Ethan did not want her crazy about him. But there was a tug of satisfaction all the same.

And then he saw the flare of curiosity in her eyes. Her hand reached out and then pulled back.

He caught her fingers. 'You touched me before...'

But she'd been lying then. And so she touched him again—tentatively this time, and without his guidance.

Had she known, Merida wondered, when she first held his hand, that she would hold him so intimately that very night?

Her amateur hand delivered bliss.

The pearl bead at his tip spread to become a silver pair, and he ground his teeth at the hunger he felt.

And then she lowered her head.

The tip of her tongue was a tease, and the heat of her lips elicited a moan from Ethan. How he wanted to push down her head, and how she ached for the boldness to do the same.

Lest he thrust—lest he come—Ethan raised her head up and lightly pushed her shoulder, so that she lay back, half on and half off the bed. Then he hitched her legs up and laid her straight.

Ethan looked down at her, taking in the riot of hair that splayed over the sheets. Her stomach was devoid of freckles, and he looked down further to the curls that hid the part of her he yearned to devour. She squirmed at the intimate perusal.

He leaned over her then, crawling up her body with cat-like stealth, until Merida got both his weight and a hot kiss, and in equal measure they were divine.

And then he looked down at her, and her wish was granted, for she had found out just how it felt to be in the path of his gentler gaze.

He parted her thighs and his mouth came near her ear. His ragged breathing was a delicious sound as she felt the first nudge of him at her entrance.

She squeezed closed her eyes and moved her hands to his hips, as if holding him back. But he pushed deeper in, then pulled back at her cry.

Merida could not get air into her lungs and her thighs shook at his sides. There was no slow torture with Ethan. He seared deep inside and she screamed.

So intense was the pain it was as if a mirror had broken before her eyes. And as he stilled, as she tried to gather in air, she wondered how the hell she had thought she could feign this.

When he started to move she wanted him to stop,

to give her time to adjust to the feel of him inside her. But there was no way he could *not* move.

The tight grip of her, and the heat they made, rendered it impossible for him to stay still. His body insisted that he thrust, and the fight within him was limited to trying to go slowly so he could savour it.

Ethan came up on his forearms and looked down at her, to discover her anguished look, but as he moved and gentled his strokes he watched the suffering recede.

'Never pretend,' he told her as he increased the pace.

And when her hips began to move with him, when her hands clawed at the pillows by her head, he moved her legs so they were wrapped around him.

'Ethan!'

She was screaming—not from pain, but from being taken, from being discovered, from being found.

He started to thrust harder. She felt the rhythm build and her hands left the pillows, began scraping his back.

Hot and urgent, he built within her a frenzy she never wanted to escape.

And the real beauty was his intensity.

He shattered her defences and then gathered her again, her climax so intense that she felt as if she'd left her body. And then came the velvet of his moan, and the breathless shout of his release as Ethan spilled deep inside her.

He collapsed atop her and she lay there, feeling

her senses slowly return and then the softness of his kiss.

'Never lie like that again,' he warned her.

And sated, pliant, a virgin no more, Merida nodded. For in the gentle afterglow she truly believed she never would.

Ethan *knew* her.

CHAPTER SIX

MERIDA *NEVER* WANTED to lift her head. It lay on Ethan's chest and his hand was idly stroking her arm.

There was an absence of awkwardness.

Neither pretended to be asleep, and she lay there thinking of their night.

It had been amazing.

For both of them.

The oddest thing for Ethan was that it still was.

It seemed incongruous to think that his father was right now being wheeled down to the operating theatre.

Because of that, he turned on his phone.

When it immediately rang, Ethan answered it. 'Hey.'

'Did you manage to visit the gallery?'

It was Khalid.

'I did.'

'And?'

'You have nothing to worry about,' Ethan said. 'Can I call you back later?'

'Of course.'

He lay there, thinking about all that had taken place, and winced inside when he thought of how he'd very nearly taken her standing, never for a moment thinking that it might be her first time.

'Any regrets?' Ethan asked.

'None,' Merida said, and then she amended that. 'Well, there is one.'

'What's that?' He frowned. 'Did I—?' He had been about to ask if he'd hurt her, but she smiled and interrupted him to tell him the only regret she had.

'I have to go soon.'

'Ah, yes—your audition.'

She untangled herself from his arms as a worrying thought struck. 'I left my bag and my coat in the restaurant! I *always* wear my kilt for my auditions. It will be bad luck otherwise...'

'I'll have it sent up.' He interrupted her momentary panic and picked up the bedside phone.

She lay there as he ordered breakfast too. 'I don't have time for breakfast,' she said.

'You can take it with you. I'll have them bring up some takeout containers.'

'Thank you.'

'No problem.'

As he ordered Merida couldn't help but think that he was nothing like the demon she'd read about or been warned of. She had never felt more looked after in her entire life. The way he had taken such care of both her body and her feelings last night...

'Ten more minutes,' Merida said when he pulled

her back into his arms. 'You make a very nice snooze button.'

'Push *there*,' he said, and took her hand.

She felt him tumescent beneath the sheet, but though she lingered a second, exploring him, Merida didn't trust either of them not to lose track of time and pulled away.

Ethan knew then that he had to have her back in his bed that night.

'Ethan?'

'Yes.'

'Did you book this suite before you asked me to dinner or while we were dancing…?' She looked up at him. 'Were you so certain that I'd say yes?'

'Yes,' he said. 'Then he gave her arm a squeeze to show he was teasing. 'I have a permanent suite here.'

'Oh.'

No wonder they all knew him, and his likes and dislikes.

'What's wrong with home?'

'Home's fine,' Ethan said.

It was more that he kept his home address private. Certainly no lovers were invited there, and yet he was lying here now considering doing just that.

Merida's phone beeped, but she didn't need to check to know who it was. 'That will be my friend Naomi, wishing me luck.'

'Is she here?'

'No, in England.'

'Is she an actress too?' Ethan asked, wanting to know more about Merida and her world.

'No, she's a neonatal nanny.'

'What?'

'A maternity nanny. She looks after newborns and gets them into a routine before the permanent nanny takes over.'

'I could think of nothing worse.'

Merida laughed. 'What are *you* doing today?'

'I'm not sure,' Ethan said. Usually by now he'd be showered and sitting in his office. In fact, he had a meeting at eight. 'I should call Abe…'

'Your brother?' Merida checked sleepily, remembering what she'd read about him.

'Yep.'

'Are you close?'

'We work together.'

'But are you close?'

'Not really,' Ethan admitted.

'What about with your father?'

He felt a touch of discomfort at the personal questions, but then he remembered that last night he had asked her the same.

Only it wasn't just her question that had caused discomfort to spike in him.

It was the answer.

'Not really.'

Merida looked up and met his dark eyes.

'We're too similar,' Ethan explained.

'Then I like him already.'

He hadn't been expecting that. Ethan hadn't even expected to give such an honest response, but lying in bed, relaxed and turned on, he was being more open than he'd ever been.

He lowered his head and Merida stretched her neck so that their lips met. She was loving his morning kiss. The scratch of his mouth on her chin and the promise it held... God, his kisses were potent.

Their tongues were lazy but their responses were not. She felt as if he'd hit the accelerator, because with just the stroke of his hand on her naked breast she wanted to give in to his touch and climb on top of him.

But Merida hauled herself back from the edge and peeled herself from his mouth. 'I have to get ready...'

'Pity.'

She disengaged herself from his warm strong body and climbed out of bed.

He saw the bruises his mouth had made last night, and the sight of them on her thighs served as such an explicit reminder it went straight to his groin—she smiled at the lift in the sheet.

'Want me to take care of that for you?' Merida drawled, and when he blinked at her sudden forthrightness she laughed. 'Not really. I'm just getting into the part for my audition.'

'Tease.'

Ethan watched her walk off and seriously considered following her into the shower. But he knew that time was tight and that this audition was important to her.

So he lay there, thinking not just about last night

but about the one ahead. He realised it wasn't just the night he wanted, but the day too.

Ethan checked his phone. There was still no news from his father, but he called Helene and, for the first time in a very long time, cancelled his work day.

Merida took her time showering. Though she should have been rushing, in her tiny shoebox of an apartment her shower ran hot and cold at intervals. This morning she stood under jets of delicious, perfectly temperature-controlled water, lathered her hair with a shampoo that smelt of lemongrass and soaped her body, tender from Ethan's ministrations, with a gel that smelt heavenly.

What happened next? She couldn't help but wonder… She really was so very new to all this.

Out of the shower, she squeezed the water from her hair with a thick white towel and then pulled on a fluffy white robe before heading out to find Ethan still in bed and a table laid with breakfast. The drapes had been opened and she looked out over a foggy Central Park.

There were light-as-air pancakes with mascarpone and cinnamon, and strong coffee in a takeaway cup. If she'd ordered herself Merida could not have chosen better.

'What?' she asked when she felt him looking at her as she took mouthfuls of food while going to the wardrobe. Sure enough, there was her trench coat and her bag.

'You *are* on the Pill?'

'Yes,' Merida said. She usually took it each night,

before bed, but she'd be taking it the very second she got back to her apartment. 'I use it so that I don't have to worry when I'm performing.'

'Merida…' He was about to lecture her—tell her that, in future, she shouldn't have sex without protection.

Ethan wasn't being a hypocrite; he had *never* risked it until last night. And he wanted to point out that men were basically liars, and that she should— But there his thought pattern halted, because he could not stomach the thought of her with anyone else.

She glanced over and saw his serious expression.

'Honestly, don't worry,' Merida said. 'I'm covered.'

'Good.' He watched as she ran a wide comb through her hair. 'I was thinking…'

'I am *not* coming back to bed.' Merida smiled. 'And please, please, *please* don't try and tempt me. I've a terrible feeling that I'm open to persuasion, but I really do need this job.'

She took a breath. The butterflies in her stomach were having a field-day—because not only did she have pre-audition nerves, she had an extra flock of the beautiful, nervous little creatures entirely devoted to *him*.

Having eaten breakfast, she sat on the bed and pulled from her bag her tights and bra and proceeded to put them on.

'What?' she said again, because he was still looking at her, and she could feel he still had a question on her mind.

Ethan did—and that was unheard of the morning after. Usually he was aching for a lover to leave, not considering prolonging things.

'I could come with you. Not to the audition… But I could hang around and we could go for brunch after.'

His offer was utterly unexpected.

Like a delicious jolt to her spine.

She had been bracing herself to remain dignified at their parting.

Merida pulled on her jumper, and when she'd tugged it over her head she looked out of the window to a foggy New York City morning and knew she would never forget that moment.

Ever.

It wasn't an ending.

At least not here, and not yet.

No goodbye, no holding in tears, would take place here.

She could look at the skyline and at this stunning hotel and remember for ever an utterly perfect night, because it did not end here.

'Yes,' Merida said in a voice that sounded a touch calmer than she felt. 'That sounds wonderful. I have to stop by my apartment first, for my papers and things, and to get ready.'

'Then we'd better get over to yours.' He reached for the phone. 'I'll call my driver.'

'Ethan, I'm not rocking up to my audition in a chauffeured car.'

'Why?'

'Because I'm not,' Merida stated, and pulled on a kilt made up of shades of summer. 'We'll walk.'

She looked, Ethan thought, completely stunning. Her hair, along with the bright colours of the kilt, was a delicious burst of colour on a busy morning.

They chatted as they walked quickly, headed for Hell's Kitchen, where Merida had a tiny place above a loud Italian café.

'Do you have lines to rehearse?'

'No.' Merida smiled.

'Have you been to many auditions since you've got here?'

'I only recently got my Equity card, but I've been for more auditions than I can count.'

They arrived at the Italian café, which this morning was relatively quiet.

'This is me,' Merida said, and gave Maria, the owner, a wave through the window.

Ethan had fully intended to wait outside, though he couldn't help but be curious, so he walked with her up the dingy stairs.

It was a studio apartment. There was a bed, a small kitchenette, and he guessed behind a beige door must be the bathroom. There was not much else.

She hauled out her suitcase from under the bed and sorted out the papers she might need. 'Do you think I need to take my passport?'

'I've never been for an audition,' Ethan replied. 'You're really nervous, aren't you?'

'I really am,' Merida agreed. 'I'd better tart up.'

'Tart up?'

She nodded, but didn't elaborate.

'I'll wait outside for you,' Ethan said. 'Give you some space.'

She was running late, so she headed to the bathroom and quickly got to work. There, she added loads of eyeliner and mascara, and wished that she *hadn't* washed her hair, because the bedhead look would have been much better.

She kicked off her boots and put on a sheer pair of tights. Then poked a finger through the knee.

And she was going to have to get Gemma a box of chocolates, or something, because the black stilettoes were being worn again.

A shabby bra was easy—Merida could have worn any of the ones she had in her drawer. And then she put a skimpy black top on.

There was no full-length mirror in her apartment, so Merida just had to hope she looked low-rate hookerish enough.

She clattered down the stairs in her heels, her mind too full of her audition and the waiting Ethan to remember that she had meant to come home to take her Pill. Instead, she was wondering why Ethan had chosen to wait outside. Perhaps the chaos of her tiny apartment was too much, Merida thought. It certainly wouldn't be anything like he was used to.

But Ethan hadn't left for that reason. Once outside, he had pulled out his phone. It was nine-thirty, and usually by now he'd have achieved close to two hours of work.

He'd called Abe. 'Any news?'

'Why aren't you in the office?'

'I'm taking the day off.'

'Well, I just called the hospital and he's still in theatre.'

'He was first on the list?' Ethan checked.

'He's the *only* one on Jacobs's list,' Abe corrected. Jobe Devereux would have the top surgeon's full attention for as long as was needed. 'Apparently he went down at eight.'

'Keep me posted,' Ethan said.

'Sure.'

There was no small talk.

They didn't do that.

Ethan didn't voice the maths that was going on in his head. If he'd gone down at eight, there would have been, say, half an hour till he went under. And that was being generous. Exploratory surgery? Well, there Ethan's expertise died, because he didn't have a clue.

Ethan just wanted the call to come saying that everything was okay so he could shake the black feeling that had clung to him like a murky shadow since… Well, since a couple of months ago, when he'd first seen his father wince with a pain he'd quickly denied.

And that jibe about him refusing to follow the professor's orders and only partake in a light supper? That had been for *both* their benefits—a stab at a pretence that things were normal.

But in truth, apart from soup in restaurants, Ethan hadn't seen his father eat in weeks.

He wasn't ready to lose him.

Oh, they weren't close by most standards, but Ethan had always hoped there would be time to work on all that.

He stared unseeing as a laundry truck pulled up and the world went about its day.

Please, let him be okay.

'Ready?'

He turned to the sound of her voice, though for a second he didn't realise it was Merida.

He looked down and saw torn stockings and high heels, and then she gave him a quick flash of her outfit beneath her trench coat: a black tube top and her kilt, rolled over at the waist to shorten it some more. She really looked the part.

'If we get photographed together, I'm going to outdo my own reputation!'

Ethan imagined Maurice's face if he was photographed walking through midtown, holding hands with a hooker. Which made him do something he rarely did, and certainly not something he'd thought he'd do today—he laughed.

The shadow lifted—just as it had last night.

'Where to?' he asked.

'Fifty-Fourth,' Merida said, and turned in completely the wrong direction.

He hauled her back. 'It's this way.'

They found the building where the auditions were

being held on the tenth floor, and as they stood outside he saw how pale her face was.

'Am I allowed to say good luck?' Ethan checked, because he knew actors were a suspicious lot.

'No.' Merida shook her head. 'You're supposed to say, *Break a leg.*'

'Very well.' He gave her a smile. 'Break a leg—though please don't. I'll meet you...' He looked across the street to a coffee shop. 'Over there.'

He watched her go in, a dart of colour disappearing into the crowded foyer, filled with many, well... pretend hookers. All, Ethan guessed, after the same part.

It was actually nice to have a morning off.

He read the news on his phone and waited for his brother to call.

Abe didn't call.

So he gave up reading and instead watched the door across the street, wondering what the hell was going on, because there seemed to be a load of construction workers filling the foyer now.

Perhaps the elevators were out, Ethan thought, and picked up his phone again.

There was still no word from Abe, so he called him. It went straight to voicemail.

There were more men in high-vis jackets and hard hats heading towards the building. Ethan had worked on enough high-rise building designs to be concerned. Was he sitting idly watching as some emergency unfolded while Merida was in there?

He stood and left the café, dodging the traffic as he crossed the busy street and entered the building.

There were workers everywhere—some standing chatting, others sitting reading their phones or newspapers. He was about to ask what the hell was going on when the elevator doors opened and Merida walked out.

Ethan let out a breath of relief and acknowledged to himself his concern.

'Hey!' He gave a rather grim response to the brightness of her presence and the cloud didn't lift entirely. There was a knot of unease still there. 'How did it go?'

'"We'll call you",' Merida said, and rolled her eyes as she walked out with him. 'I'd kill for a coffee.'

'Sure.'

His table was still free, his half-drunk bottle of water still there, so he ordered another, and a coffee for Merida.

'Is everything okay?' she checked.

'Sure.'

She wasn't secure enough in herself, let alone *them*, to notice his distraction and not assume he was bored, or had got fed up waiting. Or just fed up with her.

She'd grown up with that—bewildered by the bitter custody disputes and two separate parents who would fight to the last penny and breath for their time with her. Yet all too often, when that time came, Merida had felt like an inconvenience.

'I was just watching the foyer fill with construction workers,' Ethan explained. 'I thought you might have got stuck in the lift...'

'No!' Merida laughed. 'After the hooker auditions they're casting for a middle-aged construction worker...'

Ethan laughed at his own mistake, and at the small glimpse into her world, and then his phone went and he saw that it was Abe calling.

'I need to take this.'

'Sure.'

Only she didn't quite understand why taking a call meant he had to walk off.

Work, Merida told herself.

Only it wasn't.

'He's back from theatre,' Abe said by way of greeting.

'And?'

'He's talking,'

'And?' Ethan said, because although Abe wasn't one for idle words, there was nothing reassuring in his tone.

'You need to come to the hospital,' Abe said. 'Prof Jacobs is going to speak with us there. That's all I know.'

'Who *have* you spoken to?'

'Just get to the hospital as soon as you can, Ethan. I'll meet you there.'

He looked over to where Merida sat in the mid-morning sun, pouring sugar into her coffee, and Ethan knew for sure that everything was about to change.

Everything.

The circus that was his life was about to go full throttle, and he would *not* be exposing her to that. And neither did he need another witness to his grief.

Grief.

Ethan knew the news wasn't good for his father.

He'd known for a couple of months.

And now he had to face it.

He walked back to Merida. He didn't sit down— just stood over her and tried to work out what to say and decided that less was best.

His father's surgery was a closely guarded secret. The Devereux family did not discuss such things with outsiders.

And so he reverted to type.

Arrogant, aloof, closed-off type.

'Something's come up.'

She blinked and looked up at the sound of his voice. Ethan stood with the sun behind him, his face unreadable. Rather than fretting over her performance at the audition Merida had been sitting daydreaming—or rather last-night-dreaming— when his deep voice had hauled her back to Ethan in real time.

He was back to being the man she'd first met— detached and a touch dismissive and *very* keen to be gone.

'Something?' Merida checked.

'Yes. I need to head off.'

'Now?' Merida tried to keep the shake from her voice.

'Yes, now.'

And then she actually had to close her lips together to resist asking, *When will I see you? When will you call?*

'Be good,' he said.

When she stood up he went to leave, but then instead he turned back and did the oddest thing. He did up the buttons of her trench coat. The inside ones and the outer. And then he did up her belt.

'It's cold,' Ethan said.

Then, without looking back, he walked away.

And left her standing there.

'Does he know?'

Abe was the one asking the questions.

Ethan stood with his back to where the two other men them sat and stared out at the view.

He recognised the picture on the wall.

This was the same room they'd been taken to when they'd waited to see their mother all those years ago. Oh, no doubt the furnishings had changed, but that picture remained.

A night shot of Brooklyn Bridge, from Brooklyn, looking over to Manhattan.

To Ethan, it was the best view in the world—but he could not stand to look at it now. Instead he listened as the professor explained that Jobe had known for some time.

'So this wasn't exploratory surgery?' Abe checked.

'It was. I wanted to view the tumour myself and take some biopsies.'

'He's had scans?' Ethan asked, without looking round.

'Many of them,' the professor answered.

He loathed it that his father gone through all that alone, but Ethan knew why—his father would hate showing weakness or fear.

Now Ethan turned around. 'How long does he have?'

'It's hard to say,' Professor Jacobs answered. 'I'll know more when I get back the pathology.'

'We're not going to hold you to a *date*.' Ethan had a voice that could both be polite and hold warning. He wanted his question answered.

'With treatment to shrink the tumour,' the professor said, 'I'd say six months. But this is Jobe we're talking about, so I'm hopeful for maybe a year.'

Ethan did not let that sink in.

He couldn't.

And so he asked another question.

'Can we see him?'

'Sure.'

Ethan had expected a pale shadow of a man in the bed, but the stubborn mule was sitting up—albeit resting on pillows.

'You should have told us,' Ethan said.

'Don't start,' Jobe dismissed. 'It's to be business as normal.'

'How *can* it be?' Abe pointed out. 'You need to rest and…'

'I'll orchestrate my own demise, thank you. I don't want a sniff of this getting out.'

'The board has to know.'

'Not yet, they don't.'

A new voice spoke and Ethan turned as Maurice came in.

'Your father wants the move into Dubai announced first.'

And that was that.

On the morning he found out his father was dying, even then in the Devereux world business came first.

And so, on Ethan's first day off in living memory, he was back in the office by lunchtime.

'How's Jobe?' Helene asked, her eyes wide with concern.

'Good,' Ethan quipped, and then glibly lied. 'Gallstones or something. But that's just between us.'

'Of course.'

The show would go on.

For Merida, the show went on too.

Literally.

She performed at weekends and continued her work at the gallery.

But it was cold without him.

Oh, spring had burst into life, and the days grew longer and brighter, yet she shivered inside at his sudden departure from her life.

Well, not so sudden by *his* standards, Merida thought sadly. She couldn't say that she hadn't been warned.

And even when she received a call-back to say she had made it onto the TV show, her elation was tempered by the bleak space in her heart that he had left behind.

Even her best friend, Naomi, back home in England, noticed it.

'You don't sound as thrilled as I thought you would,' Naomi said when Merida called her with the news about the television part.

'Of course I am,' Merida said, and pushed her voice into an upbeat tone. 'Filming is Wednesday night...'

'Night?'

'I walk across the bridge, and then they find my body in Central Park at night,' Merida said. Naomi laughed. 'And then I have two days in the studio the following week.'

'Have you told your boss at the gallery?'

'He wasn't thrilled that I'm taking more time off.' Merida sighed. 'I think I'm going to have to give in my notice. He wants me to do another private tour on Saturday night when he knows I've got *Near Miss*.'

'You need the regular work, though.'

'I know I do, but it was always supposed to be a fall-back for my acting—not the other way around.'

'Well, think long and hard before you give it away.'

'I shall.'

'Merida?' Naomi checked. 'Are you sure that everything's okay?'

'Of course it is,' Merida attempted, but then her voice cracked.

'Merida…?'

'I met someone.'

And she told her the whole sorry story.

Well, not the *whole* story. She didn't reveal his name, and she left Naomi to work out the intimate details, it was enough for her to say it had been wonderful. She told her friend about the next morning, how they had got on so well. And that while in hindsight, yes, it had clearly been a one-night stand…

'It felt like a lot more at the time,' Merida admitted. 'I thought he felt the same.'

'Merida,' Naomi said gently. 'How long has it been since you saw him?'

'Two weeks—but he doesn't know my cell-phone number…'

'He clearly knows where you work,' Naomi pointed out. 'And, given that you went back to your apartment to get changed, he also knows where you live.'

'Yes.'

'And he hasn't made any effort to get in touch?'

'No.'

That said it all, really.

Merida had done all she could to put it behind her. To chalk it up to *in*experience as she swore never to be so foolish again.

And now she stood on the bridge, under lights to mimic the moon in a dark Central Park as the clapperboard snapped. The hotel where she and Ethan had spent that magical night was there in the background, but it was easy to put her head down and ignore it as she walked hurriedly on. It hurt too much to think about that night.

It was an agony that did not abate.

On her second Saturday without him Merida checked that her wig was secure and then dragged in air.

'Five minutes to curtain,' the stage manager called.

'Thanks,' Merida called back, glad that the performance was due to start.

Grateful for the escape.

That was what acting gave her.

Merida had long ago found that it was so much easier to play a part than to be herself. Smile here, frown there, look angry… Merida drew on her talent in real life.

When her father's new girlfriend had made it clear she didn't want a teenage Merida around, instead of showing hurt she had put on a mask. It was so much easier than revealing herself. And when her mother had remarried, and the awful Mike had treated Merida like a maid—well, that was exactly what she'd pretended to be in her head.

It had made making the beds kind of fun.

And now she got to forget about Ethan and the hurt and be Arrow for the night.

Merida landed on stage—deliberately awkward. She dusted herself down, turned, and found herself in the arms of Married Man. The audience laughed.

For the next two hours Merida forgot the hurt, forgot the pain and fed off the audience's reaction.

Or rather she *remembered* the hurt and *remembered* the pain and gave it all to her acting, simply poured it into her performance.

'You're on fire tonight, Merida!' Daryl, the director, told her at the interval.

And in the second act she set them ablaze.

Yes, it was an Off-Off-Broadway production, with probably just half of the sixty seats taken tonight, and yet for a short while she simply escaped into her part.

But all too soon it was over, and she was back in the dingy dressing room, peeling off her wig and trying to fathom the fact that it was now sixteen nights without him.

But then there was a knock at the door and finally, *finally* hope arrived.

'Someone to see you,' Daryl said. 'You might want to sort out your hair.'

'Who is it?'

'Believe me, he needs no introduction.'

Merida raked her fingers through her hair and then put on some lipstick. Her heart seemed to jump into her throat, and when there was another knock at the door she felt a little giddy from trying to remain calm.

It *had* to be Ethan.

She wondered how to play her reaction—and then halted herself as realisation hit. When they'd made love, and on the delicious morning after, she hadn't been playing a part with Ethan. For the first time in for ever she had been utterly herself.

And so she did not force a bright smile as the door opened—the last couple of weeks had left her too confused for that—and neither did she change her voice for his benefit. And so it was a little unsteady when she called out, 'Come in.'

Shy, nervous, excited, she watched as the door opened.

'Merida, your performance just blew me away!'

Merida was possibly the only actress in history who had visibly sagged when the eminent producer Anton Del Bosco introduced himself.

It was the oddest night.

For it was the night where the dreams she had dreamt for so long finally came true.

Merida had been invited to audition for the part of Belladonna in *Night Forest*—a new Broadway production due to open in the summer.

It was career gold, and once Anton had gone Merida took all the congratulations of her colleagues and went out for supper with them to celebrate.

Yet she was the only one not drinking champagne. Because she was rather certain that if she did she might break down and cry.

This, she kept telling herself on the cab ride home, was the best night of her life.

But instead of arriving home on a high, she wearily trudged up the stairs to her apartment and once there slumped in a chair with her coat still on, just staring out of the window, listening to the noise from the restaurant below and the endless sirens outside.

And then she did something stupid.

Merida went on her laptop and looked up Ethan Devereux.

He was out tonight at a gala function. The Carmody Ball, she read.

Merida clicked.

And she clicked again.

And she tortured herself over and over. Because of course—unlike her devastated self—Ethan had moved right along.

Blonde and beautiful, there was nothing to hate about the woman who had been on his arm tonight.

And was no doubt by now in his bed.

Merida felt sick.

More than that—she just made it to the toilet in time.

She knelt there, clutching the bowl with one hand and holding back her hair with the other.

Get over him and be happy, she told herself again and again.

After all, she had got what she'd come to New York City for.

She had a shot at Broadway.

Broadway!

Only the order of her heart had changed.

Broadway came second.

Ethan Devereux was now first.

She hadn't *fallen* in love with Ethan; instead she

had been lifted into it. Briefly lifted into a world that had felt brighter, lighter, just *better*, when it was shared with him.

And now the lights had gone out.

Now she had fallen.

CHAPTER SEVEN

If ever there was a cure for a broken heart, then rehearsing for a Broadway production came close.

Having served her notice at the gallery to a very moody Reece, Merida had gone straight into rehearsals six days a week. They were intense, and she should have no real time to think of Ethan.

Except she did.

More and more.

And it wasn't just that she missed him.

There was another concern.

Merida knew she had every reason to feel wiped out when she arrived home each night, but she was *more* than tired. In fact, she was completely exhausted.

Usually being around the theatre energised her, but with each passing week Merida felt her energy being sapped.

The whole cast was feeling the pressure, Merida told herself. But she was worried—dreadfully so— as she awaited her period.

It never came.

And once Sabine, who played a forest bird in the

chorus and was also her understudy, had caught Merida throwing up.

'You okay?' Sabine checked.

'Sure.'

Merida tried to be okay, but her mind kept darting back to that morning, getting changed for her audition with Ethan waiting downstairs.

And the teary mess she'd been when she'd returned to the apartment later, after he'd ended things.

Whatever way she looked at things, the one time she had really needed it Merida had missed her Pill.

After the second time Sabine caught her throwing up, Merida stopped at a drugstore on her way home, telling herself she simply could *not* be pregnant, that there just had to be another reason for her malaise.

After all, she had a part in a Broadway show and nothing, *nothing* must get in the way of that.

Except something had.

Pregnant.

Merida had paid extra for the test that actually spelled it out: P.R.E.G.N.A.N.T.

She sat in her tiny apartment, listening to the Italians shouting in the kitchen below, and wondered what to do and who she could call for advice.

Merida thought about her mother for—oh, twenty seconds. She knew her verdict already—*Don't make the same mistake as me!*

She'd glossed over things when she'd discussed her parents with Ethan, but the fact was her mother had been eighteen and straight out of school when

Merida had been born. And Merida knew she was considered her mother's biggest mistake.

She thought of calling her father, but could just imagine his wife rolling her eyes at the intrusion. No, she would not be going to her father for advice.

Her parents only wanted her around when she was babysitting. That was the truth and it hurt even now. Even with all that was going on, it hurt to sit in her studio apartment, above an Italian restaurant in another country, and admit that she wasn't just here for Broadway but to escape the hurt of being ignored.

She wondered if they'd even noticed or cared that she'd gone.

So who could she tell?

Naomi?

Merida did think about calling her closest friend. The problem was Naomi was a maternity nurse and very into babies.

She didn't want either extreme.

And so Merida found a new role to add to her repertoire—a woman in complete denial.

With opening night nearing, rehearsals had moved to twelve hours a day. There was a full costume and make-up photo-shoot for the programme, and things were starting to really come together.

Merida's costume was stunning, consisting of a black velvet dress the colour of atropa berries. Her eyes were rimmed with kohl and her lips painted a deep purple. Her hair wasn't hidden beneath a wig, though. It was curled and backcombed and fell in snaky ringlets.

After the photos had been taken she sat at the mirror, smothering on the cold cream to get the heavy make-up off, and smiled as Sabine came in.

'You look amazing,' Merida said, admiring her shimmering costume.

'I know—I don't want to take it off.' Sabine sighed as she undressed. 'Hey, do you want to grab something to eat?'

They ended up in the noisy restaurant below Merida's flat. The pasta was amazing, and it was nice to think she didn't have far to drag herself home afterwards.

'Shall we get a bottle?' Sabine asked, but Merida declined.

'I'll just stick to water. I'll sleep in otherwise.'

Sabine ordered a large glass of red, and as they twirled well-earned carbs around their forks Sabine asked another question. 'Is everything okay?'

'Of course.''

'Are you sure about that?' Sabine asked, and Merida looked up.

She could see the concern on her face.

'Talk to me, Merida.'

Yes, the acting world could be bitchy, but it was cliquey too, and they had worked closely together for weeks.

'I can't.'

'Yes, you can. How late *are* you?'

'How do you know?'

'Because we share a dressing room and I've heard you throwing up. Though that's stopped now.'

Merida nodded.

'I figured you'd had it taken care of. Merida, I'm not the only one to have noticed.'

Merida closed her eyes. If word got back to Anton she was sunk.

'Is the father in the picture?'

'It was just…' Merida gave a tight shrug. Certainly she would not be revealing his name to anyone, but when the words came they stuck in her throat. 'A one-night thing.'

One night that still had her heart in turmoil—one morning that she relived over and over in her mind, trying to see where it had so suddenly gone wrong.

It had felt like *so* much more than a one-night stand.

And it was.

The consequences were huge.

'I don't know what to do,' Merida admitted.

'That's why I suggested we get supper.'

Sabine went into her huge bag and pulled out a card. 'I saw him last year—he's really good. Not cheap, but you get what you pay for. He'll fit you in.'

She might be recommending a dentist, Merida thought. And though she appreciated her concern— she truly did—for the first time Merida wondered if she really had the single-mindedness that was required for an acting career.

'What if I don't want to go down that path?'

'Then I get my name on the playbill…' Sabine shrugged.

She said it without malice. And it was completely true.

With two weeks to go, no doubt the relatively minor part of Belladonna would go to the understudy.

But even though it was a minor part, it was major to Merida.

She thought of the glorious West End show she had had to pull out of at the last moment and was determined that an opening night would not be denied to her again.

One night.

And then she would tell Anton.

Then she would bow out gracefully.

It became her soul focus.

Merida's energy returned, and so did her form, and a couple of weeks after she had found out, once she felt a touch calmer inside, she plucked up the courage to call Ethan.

Reception took a lot of persuading, but finally she was put through to a woman called Helene.

Merida cleared her throat. 'Could I speak with Ethan Devereux, please?'

'Excuse me?'

'Ethan Devereux…' Merida repeated, wondering if her Internet search had cast up the wrong number.

'I *do* know who he is.'

Oh, she loved New Yorkers dearly, but she wasn't in the mood for this.

'Could I speak to him, please?'

'Regarding?'

'It's personal.'

'Yet you're calling him at work? And you've made a considerable nuisance of yourself with Reception.'

'Could you please let him know that Merida…?'

'Miss!'

She winced as Helene interrupted her.

'I assume you *are* a miss?'

'Yes.'

'Take it from me. If Mr Devereux wanted you to contact him, then he'd have told you how.'

It let her off the hook, Merida decided. Now she could focus on the part of Belladonna.

And Merida did so. As best she could, Merida pushed all thoughts of Ethan and her pregnancy out of her mind and put her heart and soul into the part.

One night with Ethan.

One night on Broadway.

With opening night just a week away, Merida had her final costume fitting. It was all coming together. For all the blood, sweat and tears, it was finally coming together.

Back in her dressing room there was a copy of the programme, and she and Sabine turned the pages with delight.

'Merida.' Anton popped his head into the dressing room 'Can I have a word?'

'Sure,' Merida said.

'Excuse us, please, Sabine.'

As Sabine got up and walked out Merida gave Anton a smile.

It wasn't returned.

'I just spoke to Rhoda in Costumes. She said the bust of your dress has to be let out and that you've also lost weight.'

'We've *all* lost weight,' Merida pointed out.

The entire cast had. Weeks of strenuous dress rehearsals meant they were all looking a touch leaner than when they had started.

But Anton had seen it all before.

'Don't play games, Merida. In some of your scenes you're harnessed…'

Merida swallowed.

'Insurance won't cover it.'

'Anton…'

'I want a note from a doctor, saying you're fit to perform, or you're out.'

'Anton, please,' Merida said. 'There's no reason…'

'There are a *hundred* reasons, Merida,' Anton shouted. 'There's one week until opening night. Take care of it or don't perform. You choose.'

It was a hellish week.

The doctor wasn't particularly friendly.

'The date of your last menstrual period?' he asked in a bored tone.

Merida closed her eyes as she tried to think back. 'Ages…' She couldn't even remember when. 'I was on the Pill…'

There was just a hint of an eye-raise from the doctor.

'I know that I was late taking one.'

'Well, to work out how far along you are we need that—or the date of conception…'

That was easy.

Merida gave the doctor the date.

In fact, she could have given him the very hour.

'That puts you at fourteen weeks,' the doctor said. 'You're into the second trimester…'

The doctor no doubt assumed from her tears that this wasn't a planned pregnancy. 'Have you thought about what you want to do? Because time really is getting on—'

'I'm keeping the baby,' Merida cut in. 'But aside from that I have no idea what I'm going to do.'

Not a single one.

She left the doctor with a due date of December fourteenth and forms for blood tests and an ultrasound. Back home, she broke her rule about telling no one the father's name and called her friend.

'His name's Ethan Devereux,' she told Naomi. 'He's from a big New York family…'

Merida started to explain.

'I've heard of the Devereux family,' Naomi cut in. 'Oh, my God, Merida, you need to come home and sort things out from this end.'

'I know that. I've booked a flight.'

'When?'

'Friday night,' Merida said.

She would be leaving on opening night—and that

wasn't by coincidence. Merida could not bear to be in New York City on the night the show opened and not be a part of it.

'I have to tell him, though.'

'I guess…' Naomi said.

Merida thought she didn't sound particularly convinced.

'But can't it wait till you're back in England and at a safe distance?'

'Safe distance? Naomi, I don't know if I've given you the wrong impression, but Ethan was a perfect gentleman with me.'

'For *one* night.'

Merida swore she heard the tear of the wrapper as Naomi tipped salt into the wound. The more she looked back on it, the less it felt like a one-night stand. It truly felt to Merida as if they'd been on a date.

More, it had been the best date of her life.

But if that were the case why hadn't she seen him since?

'You'd be better doing this from home. Merida, I deal with these types of people all the time.'

'"These types of people"?' Merida checked. 'You've never even met him.'

'I work for people who employ maternity nannies,' Naomi pointed out. 'I work for the supremely rich. And, believe me…' She paused.

'Go on,' Merida invited.

'They speak through their lawyers.'

Merida could hear a baby crying in the background and Naomi spoke again.

'I have to go.'

Those lusty sounds of a newborn's cries terrified Merida.

She had no money, no job, and no real idea what to do when she got back to England.

She couldn't land on her friend. Naomi went from job to job, house-sitting or staying at bed and breakfasts in between.

And she thought of herself arriving unannounced at either of her parents' homes but just couldn't picture it.

So she looked up prices for airport hotels and was suddenly angry.

Angry at Ethan Devereux, who had walked away from her without so much as a backward glance.

Furious at a man who lived such a slutty life that his PA played gatekeeper to his calls.

And as she packed her case on the day she was leaving her temper bubbled over and she tried to call again.

'Tell him,' Merida said when she heard the well-worn line that Ethan Devereux didn't take unscheduled calls, 'that Miss Cartwright is leaving for London tonight and that what comes next is *his* doing.'

'Now, listen. Don't start threatening—'

'No,' Merida said. '*You* listen. If he won't take my call, then he can deal with my lawyer.'

Big words indeed when she could barely afford a cab, but her words were borne of anger, fear and frustration, and the doctrines of her upbringing.

She had tried to speak with him face to face. Tried to sort it out with him like two rational adults.

Well, they could do it from opposite sides of the Atlantic now.

It was *his* fault!

And then Merida burst into tears, because she had never wanted it to come to that. She wanted to call Helene and retract her words, but it was too late.

And it was far too late for them.

Merida looked at the time and saw that she had to leave.

Instead of the yoga pants and baggy T-shirt that she had pulled on in preparation for the flight, Merida couldn't help but think about the gorgeous black velvet dress she *should* be wearing tonight.

In the life she was leaving behind she would be about to make her way to the theatre, where flowers would be starting to arrive for the cast.

Merida had dreamt of this day for most of her life, but instead she was hauling her suitcase down the dingy stairwell and going into the restaurant to hand in her keys.

'Ah, Merida!' Maria gave her a hug and told her she would miss her. *'Mi mancherai!'*

'I'll miss you too,' Merida said.

And she would.

Not just Maria but the whole city, which had truly won her heart.

She hailed a cab and once inside looked out of the window to the city that had been home for more than a year.

The home where she'd *almost* made it.

In a cruel twist, as if to remind her of all she was missing out on, the driver took her through the theatre district. And, rather than close her eyes, as perhaps she should, Merida looked out at the theatre. It was still a while until curtain up, but there were crowds starting to gather, all there to capture the star-studded opening night.

And, yes, flowers were starting to arrive.

It killed her not to be a part of it, Merida thought. It truly did. She would never have a chance like this again.

It would be nappies and sleepless nights and trying to juggle childcare while working at a job she didn't love.

But she would love her baby.

Merida already did love it. Had she not, then she'd be getting ready to appear on stage.

Her hand moved to the slight swell of her stomach.

It wasn't her baby's fault and she must always remember that.

Never, *ever* must her child know how hard it had been to leave her Broadway dream behind.

Never.

It was done, it was gone, and it was time to move forward now.

She would contact Ethan again from England.

CHAPTER EIGHT

The Devereux men, impossibly handsome, especially in their tuxedos, did not smile for the cameras as they climbed out of their cars and stood on the red carpet.

Abe had brought the long-suffering though ever hopeful Candice, who turned a blind eye to his numerous affairs in the hope, Ethan assumed, of a ring.

Jobe had not got back with Chantelle.

Ethan had not bothered to bring anyone.

There was no point.

Lately, since his father's diagnosis, all Ethan's dates had been taken home by his driver. Or rather, since that night with Merida. But he chose not to think of it like that.

Ethan did not do sentimental. He never had, and still swore that he never would, but being at the theatre was proving difficult tonight.

He missed her.

No, he told himself. Things had just been difficult of late.

Despite the dire diagnosis, Jobe's sheer bloody-mindedness meant that he was at his desk most days, but at least the board knew now.

As they walked down the red carpet all eyes were on Jobe. He held up to the scrutiny well, but there could no denying his dramatic weight loss. And Ethan could hear him a touch breathless as they made their way up the stairs to their box.

It was a gorgeous old theatre, and as they took their seats the audience beneath craned their necks for a glimpse of the stunning Devereux men. They funded a lot of arts projects, and Ethan had also been made aware that the lead performer and several of the chorus had come through a dance school that they sponsored.

Ethan took a belt of Scotch and then thumbed through the programme. A flash of red in the photos caught his eye.

Her hair was always a stand-out, and even with the heavy make-up he would have known her anywhere.

Ethan was quite sure it was her.

She was dressed in black and knelt over another actor, a wicked smile playing on her face.

Merida hadn't just been dreaming about Broadway. It would seem she really had made it!

He thumbed through the playbill and found her a few paragraphs down from the main leads.

Merida Cartwright—Belladonna

He read about her and found out that most of it he knew—she was from England and had an Art History and Drama degree. She had been acting since the age of twelve, when she had been cast in the chorus of a major West End production.

Ethan managed a wry smile at the omission, given he knew that she hadn't actually made it to the show.

He read on about how, since moving to New York City, she had appeared in an Off-Off-Broadway production, and then found that he was properly smiling as he read she had also appeared in a prime-time TV show.

Merida must have got the part.

He thought back to the morning of her audition and how it seemed as if that was the last time the sun had properly shone.

Yes, it had been cold and foggy that morning, but it had felt to Ethan as if the sun had shone that day.

Even if it was summer now, the world seemed grey. Work had been hellish of late, with Ethan back and forth between New York and Dubai. And, despite his brusque appearance, he *did* miss Merida.

He'd caved once and called the gallery, under the guise of ordering a rug.

After a little probing a somewhat bitter man had told him that Merida had moved on to better things, and that she'd just been using the gallery as a stepping stone.

Good for her, Ethan had thought.

There was an announcement reminding everyone

to switch off their cell-phones and he saw there was a missed call from Helene, but he chose to ignore it and turned off his phone.

If only his mind was as easy to switch off.

Ethan found that he couldn't wait for the curtain to lift and to see Merida again. He'd missed her far more than he dared to admit.

He'd take flowers to her after the performance, Ethan decided. He'd have no trouble getting backstage. And then, after the after-party, they would have a party of their own.

It had been weeks.

No, it had been months.

Four months, in fact, of sleeping alone.

Well, that ended tonight.

Ethan sat silent as the lights dimmed a notch, but then frowned when he heard another announcement.

'Tonight, the part of Belladonna will be played by Sabine...'

It made no sense.

It was her opening night on Broadway, for God's sake. No way would she miss it—unless she was sick, or she really had broken a leg. Or perhaps she was playing another part tonight.

The curtain was pulled back and the music struck up and he found that he was scouring the performers for Merida. When it was clear she was not performing Ethan knew that he could not sit through the show.

'Where are you going?' Abe frowned as his brother quietly stood.

Ethan didn't know.

He slipped out to where the drinks were being set up for the interval, but of course none of the staff there knew anything.

He thought of going backstage to find out what the hell was going on—because something was. There was no way Merida would miss this.

Instead he headed the short distance to her home, but of course there was no answer at her door Then he remembered her giving the owner of the restaurant a wave.

'Merida…' The Italian owner shook her head. 'You just missed her.'

'When will she be back?'

'No, no. She gone back to England.'

'When?'

'Tonight.'

Back out on the street, Ethan did what he always did on the rare occasions when he had no clue what to do and called his ultra-efficient PA.

'Helene, I need you to find out what flight a woman named Merida Cartwright is on…'

'She flies tonight,' Helene said.

'How do you know?'

'That's why I rang. She's called a couple of times and I've always put her off…'

'Put her off? Why didn't you put her through?'

'When did that policy change?' the assertive Helene checked. 'Am I now to put through *every* woman who calls you?'

'No,' Ethan conceded. 'So what did she say?''

'Well, she was angry. She said that she was leaving for England and...' Helene hesitated.

'Go on.'

He knew then the reason Merida had missed performing tonight. He knew it down to his bones, and what Helene said next only confirmed it.

'She said to let you know that you'd be hearing from her lawyer.'

There was a moment of silence, and not just from Ethan. It was as if every car on the street had suddenly switched off its engine, every siren dimmed and every conversation around him had suddenly stilled.

Then he snapped into business mode. 'Send me her number,' Ethan said. His voice was utterly even, despite the fact his heart was galloping.

She didn't pick up.

He spoke to Helene again as he walked to his car. 'Find out her flight details.'

'Ethan—'

'Just do what you can.' He got into the back and gave instructions to his driver. 'JFK,' Ethan said, and then wondered if she might be at LaGuardia.

'Sure...' Edmund drove off. 'Arrivals?'

'No—Departures.'

Such a horrible word, Ethan thought.

'Do you know the airline?'

'No.' Ethan gave an impatient shake of his head. 'I just know that the flight is tonight, to London...'

But so were several others.

'Gatwick or Heathrow or...?'

'I don't know!' he almost shouted, and for Ethan

that was rare. He didn't often raise his voice to get action, but his frustration wasn't aimed at his driver, more at himself. 'I've got Helene looking into it. Hopefully we'll know more by the time we get there.'

He saw the grim look on his driver's face at the lack of forthcoming information. And it was merited. Edmund was right to be concerned as there were endless terminals at the airport. Ethan lived in a world of private jets and first-class flights, where there was no standing in a long, snaking line. He simply rocked up to the private lounge and strolled onto his flight.

Tensions didn't improve when the ever-efficient Helene called back to say that Merida's cell-phone still wasn't responding. 'She might already be on board or have changed her SIM.'

'Keep trying,' Ethan said, but though his voice remained steady, hopelessness gripped his throat like a claw.

He ripped open his bow tie. As the car sped through the tunnel he raked his memory of the day he had been in her apartment and saw the tag on her suitcase in his mind's eye. Perhaps if this was the return trip of that same ticket…?

He told his driver what was hopefully the carrier of her flight. It narrowed it down—though not by much.

He just hoped to hell she hadn't already gone.

Merida was finally at the front of a very long check-in line. The airport was noisy and packed, and her flight was delayed, but finally things were moving.

She still didn't know if she was doing the right thing by heading home. Leaving was agony. Not just her career, but the life and the friends she had made.

And by leaving she was removing absolutely any tiny, slim chance that Ethan might look her up again.

He'd had months to do that, Merida reminded herself.

She had the start of a headache. Once her case was checked in she'd find a shop—though she wasn't sure what she could take that wouldn't affect the baby.

The baby!

She jolted whenever she said that to herself. It still didn't feel real.

And nor did the sound of Ethan calling her name.

'Merida!'

She turned and there he was. Impossibly beautiful, suited but with his tie undone. His black eyes met and held hers as he impatiently indicated her to come over.

'Miss…?'

She was finally being called to check in.

Ethan's eyes didn't leave hers, but in the moments before she had seen him the fact she was pregnant had been silently confirmed.

She was thin—too thin, really—but her breasts were bigger than they had been. Her hair was up in a messy bun, and her face was far too pale under the bright fluorescent lights.

It should have been a spotlight, Ethan thought to himself as he made his way over. She should have been on that stage when the curtain went up, not standing washed out with a case by her side about to leave.

'Come on,' Ethan said, as if he simply expected her to follow him out to the waiting car.

Which he did.

'I have to check in. I've got a plane to catch,' Merida said.

'Not now you don't.'

'Miss!' People were pushing past her and she was being told to move.

'I have to go.'

'Merida.'

His voice was incredibly cutting, and very firm, and she got a glimpse of the tough businessman she had heard he was.

'You called me threating lawyers.'

Now his eyes dusted her body and she squirmed under his scrutiny—but not in the way she once had. His gaze told her that he knew.

'I would say that we have rather a lot to talk about, wouldn't you?'

'Yes, we do. But I'm not like you, Ethan. I can't just get another flight on a whim.'

She didn't have the money to book another one, and it scared her to think of simply walking away from her ticket home.

'Merida, if you don't come now, heaven help

me, I'll put you over my shoulder and carry you to the car.'

He would.

Absolutely he would.

But he took a breath then, and did his best to fight fair. 'If we can't come to a suitable agreement I'll arrange another ticket home for you.'

Merida didn't know if she believed him, but she knew they at least had to try. She reminded herself of what she'd told Naomi—he'd always been a perfect gentleman with her—and so she nodded.

He took the handle of her case and negotiated it through the crowds far more easily than she had.

His car was there, waiting, and though she did not tell him so it actually felt like a relief to climb inside and have him join her. In recent weeks Merida had felt so incredibly alone.

The traffic was heavy and it was a slow drive back. They didn't speak much.

On the drinks console she could see the theatre programme mocking her.

'You were at the theatre?'

'Yes,' he responded tartly.

'Did you find out I'd got a part...?'

He saw hope flare then—that he'd found out she was performing, that he'd gone to see *her*—but Ethan quickly quashed it. Certainly he would not be revealing how it had felt to see the curtain open and her not to be there, so he was dismissive instead.

'Of course not. I'm here because I just found out from my PA about your calls.'

Only the terse edge in his voice stopped her crying. Merida did not want to be needy and emotional,
yet lately she'd felt just that.

Still, as the car snaked its way into the city, she
stared out of the window and could not stop thinking how tonight could have been.

Should have been.

Opening night! With Ethan watching. Acting her
heart out while not knowing that he was in the audience.

And, yes, she far preferred the fantasy that burst
into her mind—the one where he came backstage
afterwards. That was how it should have been.

Not this.

She felt like a refugee as they returned to the
stunning hotel, with Ethan still so dashing but Merida sans any black dress and pearls this time and
in long-haul flight gear.

'Good evening, Mr Devereux,' the doorman said.
'Madam.'

For once Ethan dealt with her luggage and waved
away the bellboy, heading straight for the elevators.
And this time it was Ethan who checked her reflection in the mirrored doors.

Pregnant.

Just as Merida must have stared at that word over
and over, it played on repeat in his mind. And then
he looked briefly at his own reflection, and thought
it odd that he looked much the same as the man who
a couple of hours ago had headed out to the theatre.

Yet, while he looked much the same, it felt as if a

thunderbolt had hit him and still hadn't quite gone to ground.

He'd never envisaged being a father.

The prospect didn't warm him or thaw him; it terrified him. He thought of the complete mess his father had made of things…of his own terrible reputation. Of his innate refusal to let anyone close to him. Where it had come from, he did not know, Ethan just knew it was there. And an emotional desert did *not*, to his mind, a good father make.

And then he heard her voice.

'It takes a bit of getting used to, doesn't it?'

He didn't answer. Ethan doubted he would ever get used to it.

He walked down the corridor, and the only indication that he wasn't quite as calm and collected as he was making out was the slight cuss he gave when the security card didn't unlock the door on his first swipe.

It was odd to be back in this suite, Merida thought as she stepped inside. The last time they had barely been able to keep their hands off each other; now they stood far apart as he poured two drinks.

'I can't have that,' Merida pointed out.

That didn't stop him. He took a drink as he looked at her, and she wished—how she wished—she could work out what was going on in his mind. He looked completely together—as if he'd just come back from a night at the theatre, rather than made a mad dash to JFK, having found out he was to be a father.

And then he asked a question. 'Is there any doubt that it's mine?'

She could have slapped him. 'Do you *really* have to ask?'

'Yes,' Ethan said. 'I really have to ask.'

By Devereux standards she was getting off lightly—DNA evidence would usually be required before they even met face to face.

He'd been through this before. Not directly, but with Abe. It had turned out that the baby wasn't his.

There had also been a few pregnancy scares over the years with his father, though all that had eased off in the last decade.

'Is it mine?' he asked again.

'Yes,' Merida said. 'There's been no one else before or after that night. I was a *virgin*, Ethan,' she pointed out.

'You said you were on the Pill. That you had it "all covered".' He put his fingers up and mimed quotation marks, because he had replayed that morning several times.

'I *was* on the Pill,' Merida said. 'I used to take it at night. I thought that I'd be home to take it.'

Merida looked at his rigid, unreadable face. Her voice rose to a near shout.

'I meant to take it when I got changed for the audition, but I forgot, and then, after you ended things, I was upset.'

'And now you're angry and threatening lawyers?'

'I only said that because I couldn't get through to you.'

'Well, you're through to me now.' He gave a black smile. 'Why the wait, Merida? We could have been having this conversation three months ago.'

'I only recently found out…' she attempted, but then decided it was best not to lie. 'I've been avoiding facing it.'

'Why?'

'Why do you think?'

'I'm not here to play guessing games. Why have you been avoiding facing it and telling me?'

'Because as much as I didn't want to be pregnant, I didn't want an abortion. Something told me that that might be your suggestion.'

He said nothing to that.

'And I was getting it from all angles at work.'

Still he said nothing, and she looked at his granite features.

'Why are you acting so cold?'

'I'm not acting,' Ethan retorted. 'I *am* cold, Merida.'

'No, you're not. That night we met—'

'I wanted you in *bed*!' he retorted. 'I can be charming if I want.'

'So you were *faking* being nice?' Merida let out an angry incredulous laugh. 'What about the next morning?' It still killed her the way he had ended things. 'Were you pretending then?'

He could not bear to think about that morning, so he got back to this night. 'When are you due?'

'December the fourteenth.'

This year. He would be a father *this* year.

'I don't know what to do,' Merida said, and the panic in her voice sounded a lot like the way he felt.

Yet he remained calm on the surface. 'We are where we are.'

'What does that even *mean*?'

That he would deal with it. In the same methodical way he dealt with any drama that landed on his desk.

Emotions were not helpful when it came to decision-making, and his head and his heart were both pounding now. He was looking at the night they had met through less than rose-coloured glasses now, and wondering if Merida was quite as innocent as she made out.

Sure, she'd been a virgin in the flesh—but, hell, had she seen an opportunity? Arrogance might have a part in his thought process, but it was more than that. For as long as he could remember he'd been warned to be more than careful. Mothers had deliberately enrolled their daughters in the same schools as him, young women had switched to Columbia when they'd found out he was there, just for a shot at the Devereux name.

But rather than accuse he decided to get out.

'I'm going to go,' he told her. 'Right now I think you need to rest, get some dinner...'

'You're going to *go*?' She was aghast. 'You've just found out that I'm pregnant and you're walking off...?'

'Yes,' Ethan said. 'Or I might say something I regret.'

'Such as?'

He gave a terse shake of his head. 'We'll speak tomorrow. You've had months to get your head around the fact there's a baby on the way. I've had a couple of hours, Merida. It needs to sink in.'

He needed a clear head, and so too did she—though there was one thing that had to be said.

'I would never have asked you to have an abortion.'

She just stared.

'But I would never have chosen this situation either.'

'And you think *I* would?'

He refused to be drawn. 'Get some sleep,' Ethan said. 'I'll be back tomorrow, after I've spoken to a few people.'

'Speak to *me*!' Merida shouted, and then all the weeks of pent-up fear and anger erupted. She ran at him, but Ethan was less than impressed with her drama.

'I shall be back tomorrow, and we'll work out how to proceed.'

He made it sound like a court case, Merida thought as the door closed on him. A delay in proceedings. Temporarily adjourned.

Yet as her anger faded she was actually grateful for the reprieve…

Merida opened the curtains to a gorgeous summer night and lay in bed, looking out to the park and remembering filming there and walking across the bridge, never thinking she would see Ethan again.

Let alone be back in this suite.

'We are where we are.'

Those words had angered her when he'd said them, yet oddly they comforted her now.

Ethan knew.

They would move on from there.

CHAPTER NINE

ETHAN DIDN'T GO HOME.

Instead he landed on Abe, who had a stunning brownstone in Greenwich Village.

He took for ever to answer the door.

'Sorry to disturb you.'

'No problem.'

'Tell Candice—'

'She's not here,' Abe said. 'I took her home. Come in.'

'How was Jobe?' Ethan asked as Abe poured them both a Scotch. They often referred to their father by his name; it worked far better in meetings.

'He stuck it out right to the end, but he was pretty wrecked by the time it was over. I've just been looking at the press write-ups. His weight loss hasn't gone unnoticed.'

'Well, it wouldn't, would it?' Ethan said. 'He must have lost thirty pounds. Why can't he just step back?'

'According to him, now's not the time. Anyway, you're not here about that, are you?'

'Nope.' Ethan looked over to his brother, and for

a moment wondered about the wisdom of coming to Abe for advice.

Abe, even by Ethan's standards, was a rake. God alone knew how Candice put up with him. Then again, Abe was brilliant, and tonight Ethan needed his brain.

'I met a woman some time back. The night Jobe first went in to hospital…'

'How long have you been seeing her?'

'Just that night,' Ethan said, and took a drink. 'She's from England.'

'And…?' Abe pushed.

'I've just found out that she's pregnant.'

'I hope you've told her that there's no way it can be yours.'

Ethan said nothing.

'And there is no way it *can* be yours because you wouldn't be so idiotic as to have unprotected sex…'

When Ethan still said nothing Abe let out a frustrated cuss. Then he shook his head and gave a dismissive wave of his hand.

'Get a DNA test, talk to Maurice—'

'It's mine,' Ethan said.

'And you know that because…?'

'I just know it is.'

'Does she work?'

'She's an actress.'

'So she's had *training* at being convincing?'

Ethan knew why he'd come then. Abe was like a black mirror, voicing his doubts. Yet he found himself arguing back at him.

'She was working at a gallery when I met her. I

dropped in to check things out for Khalid. Merida gave me a private tour.'

'So it would seem.'

'It wasn't like that.'

'It was *exactly* like that,' Abe said. 'And don't forget it for a moment. She saw you coming. Or rather she saw dollar signs and made sure you were coming. Some two-bit actress saw her chance—'

'Hey!' Ethan roared. 'Merida's good at what she does. I found out last night that she'd been cast in *Night Forest*...'

But it didn't sway Abe. 'I'll bet this house that she hadn't been cast when you bedded her.'

Ethan might be cynical where relationships were concerned but Abe was contemptuous.

He was also right.

'So what do you want to do?' Abe asked.

'I don't know, but I have to sort something out. She was on her way back to England when I found out.'

'Well, that sounds like a solution to me.' Abe shrugged. 'Pay her off, set her up, drop in now and then, be seen to do the right thing...'

His final words were like a punch to the gut. Ethan practically felt Abe's fist land and was grateful he was sitting down. He sat there, staring into the amber fluid, remembering being lined up for photos, smiling for journalists, being 'seen to do the right thing', just as Abe described.

And then their father, being his usual arrogant self, closing the door on his study the moment the photographers and reporters were gone.

His mind cast around for their mother, for the perfect childhood he had had before she was gone. For a memory of her.

Except there wasn't one.

Not one that he could remember, aside from the photos that lined his father's walls.

'I don't want them in another country,' Ethan said, and that winded feeling stirred into nausea as he thought of his close call tonight.

Had he arrived a few moments later they might be on a plane now.

They.

Merida and his baby.

'Then we'll sort it,' Abe said. 'It's going to cost you, but…'

'I'm not here for financial advice,' Ethan said. 'I'm thinking of marrying her.'

Ethan didn't exactly expect his brother to jump up and shake his hand and slap his back, but at the revelation that he was about to be a father Ethan had expected a little more,

But Abe was thinking in dollars. 'A contract needs to be nutted out properly. How many divorce meetings have we sat through? How many times have we stepped in when Jobe got too generous…?'

Ethan closed his eyes.

'It's not all bad,' Abe said. 'If she's an actress she'll at least know how to smile for the cameras. And it might be a nice way to divert the press from Jobe's health, or lack of it. Babies are good for that.''

'I don't know how Candice puts up with you.'

'She puts up with me because I *pay* her to,' Abe said, and Ethan looked up as for the first time he heard the truth about his brother and Candice. 'It's a business arrangement.'

'*Just* business?'

'Yes. Candice gets an apartment, a monthly allowance, and for that she just has to trot out for dinner or the theatre once in a while—and, of course, appear to forgive me for my indiscretions. The board likes to see stability and a constant partner by my side. It's not for ever. I don't doubt that I'll have to work out alternative arrangements soon. But for now everyone's happy.'

'You don't have a baby on the way, though.'

'Which makes it all the more important that you go into this well informed. Call Maurice now and tell him to meet you at the office—and to get Lewis in.'

Lewis was their contract attorney, and had had his work cut out with Jobe's health crisis.

It would seem the baton had been handed back to Ethan.

'Now?' Ethan checked.

'Now.' Abe nodded. 'Don't speak with her again until you've sorted out a plan.'

It was the classic Devereux modus operandi—they never walked into a meeting unarmed. And they *never* played nice.

'It's up to you to make it work,' Abe said. 'Set the tone from the start. You need to plan for the day when this sham of a marriage is over.'

CHAPTER TEN

ETHAN KNOCKED ON the door to his own suite and then let himself in.

There were dishes on the table when he put down his briefcase, so he knew she'd had dinner. And there were towels on the floor when he walked into the bedroom.

There Merida lay, on her side, her red hair so long that it spilled onto both pillows, her breathing deep and even.

She looked so peaceful that after a long night with Maurice and Lewis he wanted to flick the *Do Not Disturb* switch, undress and climb into bed. Not even for sex, but just to blot out the world and share in a slice of that peace.

There would be no peace today, though.

He'd listened to Lewis, but—like his father before him—had insisted on more generous terms than he'd recommended.

God, the apple really didn't fall far from the tree, Ethan thought. And then he thought how his own parents' marriage had ended—with his mother running off and dead within a couple of weeks.

He and Merida had to be properly prepared for the end of their marriage. To Ethan, that was the one certainty in all of this—because he knew, beyond doubt, that nothing lasted.

There was not one relationship that he could draw on that said otherwise. Not a single one.

It was easier to believe he'd been trapped than to believe in the beauty of that night. It was safer that way.

'Merida?'

She didn't move.

'Merida…' he said again, and watched her green eyes open and a slight moment of disorientation flick over her features as she looked up at him and first frowned and then smiled.

'For a moment I thought you were an air steward with breakfast.'

He didn't smile.

'And that I'd been upgraded to first class.'

'You have been.'

Merida sat up, and he saw that she'd gone to bed wearing the hotel robe.

'How did you sleep?' Ethan asked.

'Far better than I expected to,' Merida admitted. 'You?'

'I didn't,' Ethan replied, and she saw then that he was wearing the same suit he'd had on last night and had dark violet smudges beneath his eyes.

He called Room Service and ordered strong coffee. Merida asked for tea.

'Do you want to get dressed?' Ethan suggested. 'Before we start?'

Merida gave a small nod of her head.

'Fifteen minutes, then. I'll see you out there.'

'You make it sound like a business meeting.'

He gave a mirthless laugh and headed out of the bedroom. He didn't tell her that was exactly what this was.

Merida climbed out of bed and went through her case—although, given her expanding waist, she wasn't exactly spoiled for choice. She washed her face and settled for a pale shift dress, and then, hearing breakfast arrive, she tied back her hair and headed out.

He held a chair for her at the gleaming walnut table, and she nibbled on a pastry as he went to his briefcase.

Given that it felt like a business meeting, Merida decided that she would kick things off. She'd been doing a lot of thinking last night as she had lain looking out at the moon drifting across the sky.

A *lot*.

'I'm not asking for financial support...'

For some reason that served to make him smile, she saw. Not a friendly smile, though, more a private smile—as if she had delivered the punchline to some private joke.

But Merida pushed on. 'I want to work.'

'As an actress?'

'Yes,' Merida said. 'Well, once the baby's old enough, of course.'

'And who's going to look after the baby while you work?'

Merida swallowed. 'I won't be the first mother to work.'

'You'd be the first Devereux wife who did,' Ethan said, and then shook his head. 'The only solution is marriage.'

'Ethan…' She shook her head in turn. 'It's the twenty-first century. We don't have to get married.'

'I don't care what century it is,' he responded. 'I'd like my child to have my surname. And I'd like my baby to be born here. Now, we both know this isn't a love-match…'

He just said it as fact, unaware of the sting his words delivered, and he continued speaking, oblivious to the tears in her eyes.

'Neither of us will be going into this with stupid illusions.'

'Love can grow…' she said hopefully.

'We're not plants.' Ethan tossed her notion aside.

'No, but remember the amulets…'

His lips parted, but before he could give a derisive laugh she spoke again.

'What I meant is that arranged marriages often work well…'

'Then let's arrange it well.'

'That's not what I meant either.'

'I know that—but listen to me.' He was firm. 'I don't believe in love, Merida. More than that, I don't even want to test the notion.'

He wanted to be drawing up a contract—not sitting drinking coffee as they discussed some imaginary castle in the sky. Ethan never *ever* wanted the responsibility of another's heart, nor any foolish belief in love.

He had grown up guarding his heart and there was a wall of steel clamped around it now, for he had to keep his head in this.

'What about the baby?' Merida asked. 'What happens to our baby in this loveless world of yours?'

'I can't answer that,' Ethan said through gritted teeth, 'because I haven't met our baby yet. Merida, what the hell did you expect? We hooked up one night and, as good as it was, it's not really a recipe for longevity.'

He took a breath and tried to push aside the memories of just how good it had been, reminding himself that sex was the easy part.

'Listen, Merida. You look after yourself, I'll look after myself, and together we will do the very best by our child.'

'You're talking about a business arrangement?'

'Absolutely.'

'And in this *arrangement* do we sleep together?'

'I believe a marriage has to be suitably consummated,' Ethan said, and then grew irritated at her pointless question. 'Of *course* we'll sleep together.'

'Even though we don't love each other?'

'You can put your moral compass away now, Merida. You didn't seem to mind too much a few months ago.'

She folded her arms, angry at his words and wanting to refute them. It hadn't felt like a hook-up. How bloody dared he? Yet she guessed, to him, that was all it had been.

'Don't worry,' Ethan said as he handed over the contract. 'If either one of us cheats it will be an expensive mistake.'

He was covering all the bases as he shredded her heart.

'We've given this a lot of thought...'

'We?'

'A select few members of my team have been working with me through the night.'

'Talking about us?' She was up on her feet now. 'Last night I asked that you speak to *me*...'

'Merida.' His calmness only accentuated her drama. 'Sit down and tell me what *you* think we should do.'

She sat down. 'We could...get used to the idea. Together. Maybe date...'

'So you'd stay here in New York?'

'Yes.'

'And where would you live?'

Merida swallowed. 'You have this suite here...' she said, and then winced a little as he dragged out of Merida her flimsy plan.

'Okay, so I house you in a five-star establishment. I presume you'd need an allowance—how much?'

'I'll get a job,' Merida retorted.

'Yes, because finding a job when you're pregnant is *so* easy.'

'I'll go back to the gallery,' Merida attempted,

but then sagged. She doubted Reece would have her back. 'Or I'll get a job waiting tables.'

'And then come back and sleep here at night?' From across the table he gave a mocking laugh. 'What about medical care? I'm presuming your holiday insurance won't cover it?'

'No,' Merida said, because she'd already looked into that. 'You'd pay for my medical care and the care of your child.'

'Who I'll be housing in a hotel?' Ethan wasn't laughing now—he was deadly serious. 'Have you any idea how ridiculous that sounds? Don't you see that we need a properly drawn out plan? One that covers both of us? Because from where I'm sitting, you hold all the cards.'

'Me?'

'If I don't adequately take care of you there's nothing to stop you from getting on a plane and leaving...'

He closed his eyes for a second, for his mother had done exactly that. But this was different, Ethan told himself.

'A marriage, properly arranged, will take care of all of us.'

He moved on to the next item. And he actually hadn't said this out loud to anyone.

'My father's not well,' he said, and then elaborated. 'It's terminal.'

'I'm sorry.'

'No one is allowed to know yet,' Ethan warned.

'Oh, and there was me about to ring down to Reception and tell them.'

He didn't smile—he just stared.

'I was being sarcastic,' Merida said, and then closed her eyes, because a sarcastic response perhaps wasn't the best one when he'd just told her his father was going to die. 'Of course I'm not going to say anything. How long have you known?'

'It doesn't matter.'

Oh, but it did. In their time apart it would seem that so much had happened.

'As I said,' Ethan continued, in such cool business tones that she half expected to look over and see someone else sitting there, taking notes. 'A grandchild on the way will certainly make things...' He snapped his fingers as he searched for the words.

'It might give your father some hope—something to look forward to?' Merida offered.

'I was thinking more of the shareholders. It will show them some stability.'

If there was any precise moment when he became a stranger to her, then that was it. But she had been warned about how cold and calculated the Devereux family were. It shouldn't come as a surprise to find out that everything she'd read and been told was right, yet it did.

'Who *are* you?' Merida demanded. 'What happened to the man I met...?'

'The man you met was having a night off from himself!' Ethan retorted angrily. '*This* is who I am. Perhaps you should have done your research a bit better before you—'

'Go on,' Merida invited.

'It doesn't matter.'

'It does to me.'

'Fine. You were a struggling actress when I met you, Merida. If I remember rightly "nearing desperation" were your words about yourself. I'm not saying you set out to get pregnant, but I don't think you exactly rushed to take your Pill.'

He felt a flicker of guilt when he saw her already pale face bleach.

In truth, that day, walking away from her, hearing his father was dying... Well, he'd forgotten even to eat until the next day, let alone take some damned pill.

But he would not back down. This was too important for sentiment to get in the way.

'I'll never forgive you for that, Ethan.'

'That's okay,' he said. 'I don't need your forgiveness, nor a life spent living a charade.'

He told her they would be divorced after one year, and then spoke of allowances and apartments, rattling off details as she sat there stunned.

'I don't want the first months of our child's life spent with us hammering out details through attorneys on either side of the Atlantic. By the time our marriage is over we'll have hopefully come to an arrangement that works for both of us.'

Merida felt her breathing turn shallow.

Yes, she might have fired the first 'lawyer' shot, but being mired in a custody dispute was the last thing she wanted for her child. She'd been mired in her parents' disputes for years.

Ethan was right—he was a complete stranger, but he was right. They *had* to do what was best for the baby, and right now that meant her staying here.

And to do that she needed his financial help.

But marriage…?

'I want my child to have my name,' Ethan reiterated. 'And, given my father is dying, I'd like to think the baby could be born here and…'

He didn't finish. In fact, Merida thought she heard a slight husk to his voice. But when she looked up his expression was as stony as ever, and she decided she'd misheard.

'Take your time,' Ethan said.

Merida read through the contract, but the words blurred.

Suddenly she'd become *the aforementioned*. Their baby *the dependant*.

She didn't need to read through all the pages to guess there would be no mention of love.

'Do you have any questions?' Ethan asked, just as he had on the night they had met.

But there was no suggestive edge there now. No seamless move to invite her to dinner. Or to bed.

Not that she'd go.

Merida felt utterly wiped.

'None.'

'If you can give me your parents' contact details I can let them know that I'm happy to organise their attendance. Helene will sort out flights and accommodation.'

Merida nodded.

'I think that's everything, then.' He stood.

A huge tear rolled down her cheek, followed by another. And though in her line of work Merida had been taught to cry on demand, she must have missed the class where they were taught how to stop, for the tears would not stop falling.

'Stop the crocodile tears, Merida.' His voice was like ice.

'They're *not* crocodile tears!' Merida gulped, but Ethan had clearly decided they were.

'And don't worry about giving up your career,' he added when she had signed the papers and he was clearing up. 'You just landed the biggest gig of your life.' Ethan gave her a black smile. 'Playing the part of my loving wife.'

CHAPTER ELEVEN

ALL BRIDES WERE nervous on their wedding day. But Merida felt as if she might pass out.

It was to be a true whirlwind wedding.

They'd got their marriage licence first thing on Monday and now, on Tuesday, Merida stood in Ethan's suite with her teeth chattering as she was preened and readied for the role of her life.

'I'd like to wear my hair down,' Merida attempted, but Howard the stylist had other ideas—it would be smoothed and worn up.

And when she looked at the rack of stunning dresses that several bridal houses had sent up, and her hand lingered on a dusky lilac peplum dress that would surely disguise her bump, Howard snatched it out of her hands in horror and told her how it would be.

'You're marrying a *Devereux*, my dear—not joining the circus.'

Her red curls were smoothed to become glossy and straight, and then coiled into an elegant French pleat. Her nails were buffed and painted nude, as were her lips.

And the dress chosen for her was a very pale gold.

'I'm not sure…' Merida said as she stood looking at her unfamiliar reflection, but Howard and his cronies seemed incredibly pleased.

'It's perfect,' Howard insisted.

The dressers and the stylist left, and when there was a knock on the door she opened it to the stunning sight of Ethan.

'You look wonderful,' he said, though privately he thought she looked like a sepia photo—dimmed and toned down.

'Thank you,' she answered. 'You do too.'

Ethan actually did. His charcoal-grey suit was immaculate and he wore a gunmetal-grey tie. He was utterly clean shaven, as of an hour ago, and yet a raven-blue hue lay beneath the surface.

'Isn't it bad luck for us to see each other before the wedding?'

'I already told you—I'm not superstitious. Anyway, I need to give you this. It was just delivered.'

'Oh…?'

He put his hand in the pocket of his suit and produced a ring.

No box.

No speech.

No moment.

A stunning emerald-cut diamond was handed to her, but when Merida's eyes glittered it was with tears. She refused to let him see them—she would not be accused of faking it again.

'When you're asked where I proposed—'

'We've been through this, Ethan,' Merida said, pushing the ring on. 'We met at the gallery where I worked...' They hadn't actually deviated much from the truth—more extended the timeline.

There was no pretence at romance. Absolutely none.

They took the elevator down, and just when she wanted to turn and bolt back up to the suite he took her hand.

'Come on. Let's do this.'

He sounded as if he was on the way to his own funeral.

It was to be a City Hall wedding—where, Ethan told her, it was first come, first served.

There, they stopped by a desk and took a number, and were told that the wait was around two hours.

'Plenty of time, then,' Ethan said.

'For what?'

'You'll see later.'

Ethan was quite confident that word would have spread to the press by the time they were finished with the ceremony.

City Hall was, Merida soon discovered, a rather wonderful place to pass the time. There were cheers and tears, families and friends. But theirs weren't there.

Merida could not think about her parents now, so she watched the anxious brides and tense grooms waiting to marry, though some seemed relaxed and simply enjoying the day.

Ethan sat and occasionally tapped a well-shod

foot, and in her chest butterflies leapt, but apart from that they might well be sitting in a doctor's waiting room.

'The photographer will be here soon,' Ethan said. 'He's our witness.'

'I see.'

She didn't really.

Merida watched a couple come out. The woman was heavily pregnant, and as she watched their loving embrace Merida felt sure that she and Ethan would never be like them.

'Having second thoughts?' Ethan asked.

'Yes,' Merida admitted. 'Are you?'

'No,' Ethan said.

He had given it enough thought to feel positive that this was right. In fact, he'd feel a whole lot better once this was all made legal.

'We're up,' Ethan said.

They walked in for their two-minute wedding ceremony, and though she had been expecting very little, it was incredibly nice.

The celebrant was a real New Yorker, and clearly thrilled to be a part of this day.

'Mr Devereux, this is a pleasure!' he boomed. 'And Miss Cartwright—can I say that for the last time?'

Merida found that she laughed.

She did make a very beautiful bride, Ethan thought. Her lipstick was the coral one she had worn when they met, and a curl of red hair had escaped and fallen over her face. He pushed it to the side.

'We've got this,' he told her.

On a day when she felt as if a flock of seagulls were roosting in her chest, and when it took all her focus and acting skills to appear calm and smile, there was an almost surreal moment when they exchanged rings that she felt they might just get this right.

'You may kiss your bride.'

Ethan did so—and it had been such a very long time since he had kissed her.

It was measured, and it was more sensual than tender. Ethan's hands held her bare arms as he kissed her, long and slow, and she was glad of that, for at his lips' command her hands wanted to lift to his head. And if she couldn't do that, then she wanted to rise on her tiptoes, to press harder to his mouth.

But she didn't. In fact she fought with her body *not* to respond—to simply kiss as she would were she on stage.

The photographer was clicking away and Merida, whose mind had been only on their wedding day, now moved on to thinking of their wedding night.

And as Ethan released her his black eyes and subtle smile told her he was thinking of the same thing.

He had been so abrasive, so cold at their meeting, that she had expected the same from his kiss.

Oh, she should have asked more questions about their contract when he'd invited her to do so, but she hadn't been able to bear it.

Now Merida wanted a time-out. Just a moment to work out how she was going to deal with the quivering wreck he made her and somehow hold onto her heart.

This was a business arrangement—one she had agreed to so that they would be in the same country at least when their baby was born, and would share in that valuable time.

Yet his kiss had rocked her world.

And now there was no more time to think. For she was Mrs Ethan Devereux, and Merida found that their supposedly *low-key* wedding had been completely staged to be anything but.

In the hours they had sat waiting word had got out and the press had gathered. She felt as if every tourist, every native New Yorker, was watching as Ethan Devereux once again took his bride in his arms.

The photographer positioned them on the iconic steps of the court building and she felt Ethan's hand warm on the side of her waist. And then they turned so they faced each other and she looked up into his dark eyes.

'Hello, wife,' Ethan said, which made her smile.

'Hello, husband.'

Merida was shaking a little, although not from nerves—she could play to an audience, after all. It was his touch that made her shiver. And the fact that they were together and locked into a contract that, for this moment, didn't feel like a lie.

He blocked the sun and yet he lighted her world. And when their lips met again she forgot the ruse, forgot the savage terms of their contract, and knew why she had agreed to marry him. It wasn't for the shareholders, or for a father who was ill, and nor was it to give their child a stable home.

She had married him with hope in her heart.

Hope that what they'd so briefly found on the night they had met might somehow return.

A foolish hope, perhaps, but it was all she had.

'What happens now?' Merida asked as they descended the steps towards the car.

Their quiet, intimate wedding was fast becoming anything but. There were barriers up in the street, and the NYPD were between them and the crowd.

'Do we go back to the hotel now?'

'We're going there.'

Always he surprised her. Instead of agreeing that they were heading back to the hotel for more photos, Ethan was nodding towards the beautiful Brooklyn Bridge.

'For more photos?' Merida asked.

'No, just dinner with a few family and friends,' Ethan said as they got into the car. 'Merida, I *did* try and organise for your parents to be here.'

She felt her throat tighten.

'It's the school holidays, though, and—'

'I know.' She halted him. 'They already had plans.' Merida was very used to their new families coming first.

'Merida...'

'It's fine.' She gave him a tight smile. 'You know, there are advantages to a whirlwind wedding. I always dreaded having them in the same room.'

It was, Merida thought, the loneliest wedding in the world. Aside from the fact that the groom didn't love her, her parents were too busy with their lives to be here.

'Why don't you call them now?' he suggested, but she shook her head.

'They might hear that I'm upset, and I have no desire to let them know how hurt I am that they didn't try to get here.' She looked over. 'It's just as well this marriage isn't—'

'Eduard!' He stopped her from saying the words out loud. 'How about you take a photo of us here?'

It was no doubt completely illegal, but Eduard asked the driver to pull over and they got out.

'I'm sorry about that,' Merida said, appalled that less than an hour in she had already messed up.

'Just know that every time you break our cover I will silence you with a kiss…'

Another kiss, another tease…another moment she would have to erase when she attempted to put her heart back together.

She would get through today, Merida decided as they got back in the car. And then she would get through tonight…

'When do you go back to work?' Merida asked.

'The day after tomorrow,' Ethan answered. 'Why?'

Because then she would be able to breathe…then she would be able to think. It was impossible to do that with him near.

'We're here,' he told her.

'Here' was an extremely elegant riverboat, and as

they entered they were greeted with smiles and led straight through.

Nothing could have prepared her for the view. The whole of Manhattan glittered before them, and the bridge they had just been on stretched over and ahead like a golden rainbow.

Their table was by the window, cordoned off, but as they walked through the boar there were smiles from all the other patrons, delighted to find themselves inadvertently at such an exclusive event.

Their table was dressed with candles and gardenias, and the invited guests stood with glasses raised as the very new couple approached.

'Merida,' Ethan said, 'this is my father, Jobe...'

'Meredith,' he said.

'Merida,' Ethan corrected, with a slight roll of his eyes, but Merida just smiled. She was used to people getting her name wrong.

'You're a brave woman,' Jobe said, 'taking us lot on.'

'Apparently so,' Merida replied.

'This is my brother, Abe...' Ethan almost needlessly introduced them, because the brothers were both as dark and good-looking as each other, and neither readily smiled.

'Merida,' said Abe, and gave her a kiss on the cheek. 'This is my partner, Candice.'

Candice was tiny and shockingly beautiful, with caramel blonde hair and diamonds at her ears and throat, but the smile on her lips did not meet her china-blue eyes.

'Merida!' Another air-kiss, and then the sting of words only Merida could hear. 'We've heard so *little* about you.'

Candice made Abe seem welcoming! But Merida didn't have time to find out what Candice's problem was because there were more people to meet.

'This is the Sheikh Prince of Al-Zahan,' Ethan said. 'Or Khalid.'

Merida swallowed. Though he was in a suit, still he had the presence of a royal sheikh prince—and Merida knew that name…

'It is a pleasure to meet you, Merida,' said Khalid. 'I believe I can take the credit for introducing the two of you?'

'It's *your* mother's amulets on display at the gallery!'

'Yes, I like to keep an eye on things and I asked Ethan to drop in. I trust his judgement. He said they were being looked after beautifully.'

Merida forced a smile. It stung that their meeting had been a set-up—that Ethan had been testing her on the night they had met.

When they had taken their seats, and everyone was chatting amongst themselves, she turned to Ethan. 'You were testing me.'

'When?'

'On the night we met. Khalid said you came to check up on the amulets.'

'Yes.' He made no attempt to dress it up. 'Khalid had heard that the gallery wasn't doing the display justice. He'd sent in a couple of people to check it out discreetly, but before he pulled the display he wanted to know my thoughts.'

'So you had no interest—?'

'Merida,' he cut in. 'Do I *look* like someone who's interested in Egyptian dolls' houses?'

It upset her—possibly more than it should. But the fact that their chance meeting had been anything but left a bitter taste in her mouth.

Ethan, though, was unperturbed. 'It's no big deal,' he said, and got back to speaking with the guests.

It was to Merida.

There was small talk and chatter, and delectable food, but although she tried to fit in Merida felt like an outsider. The rings on her finger felt unfamiliar, and she could feel the scrutiny of Candice's constant gaze.

She made it through the starter, and then the main courses came out.

'It was sensational,' Jobe was saying. 'What a night!'

It took her a moment to realise they were talking about *Night Forest* and the night she had almost had.

'Merida…' Jobe turned to her. 'Ethan said that *you've* done some acting?'

He was trying to draw her in but had inadvertently frozen her out, because it hit Merida then that these people didn't know her at all. And there was no real point in them doing so when three hundred and sixty-four days from now she would no longer be a part of this family.

So, when her face felt as if it might freeze from smiling, she decided that an interval was called for.

'Excuse me…'

She found the restrooms, but on her way back, instead of going to the table, she turned and headed out to the platform, and looked at the gorgeous view.

She could see the Statue of Liberty, all lit up. The wind whipped her hair and she felt like crying. And then she nearly did cry, because for the first time ever she felt her baby move.

The little flutter inside wasn't a kick, but it felt like a bird stretching its wings. And it was the only reason that she and Ethan were temporarily together.

Oh, where was a tissue when you needed one?

'Getting some air?'

It was Jobe, and she quickly wiped her face with her hands and then turned and forced a smile as he came over.

'I just said to Ethan, Where's your bride? Is it over already?'

She knew in that moment that Jobe was aware it was all a farce. No doubt he had had to approve the contract.

It dawned on her then that *everyone* at her wedding probably knew. They were the inner circle. The very select few.

Jobe came and stood beside her. 'I used to bring Abe and Ethan to the pier when they were little. We'd get pizza and watch the world go by.'

'A family day out?' Merida kept her smile pasted on her face.

'Oh, Elizabeth didn't come. It wasn't all gentri-fied around here then. No, just me and the boys. Not often, mind… I was always working. Still am.'

She really looked at him then. He was probably sixty, and with streaks of silver in his black hair he was elegant and handsome. To Merida's surprise, he was kind, too. For not only had he come to check on her but he now took out a handkerchief and gave it to her.

'Thank you.'

'Emotional things, weddings,' Jobe said.

'Yes.'

'I bet your family's upset to miss it,' he said, and when she started to cry again he added. 'Whoops, I've set you off.'

'It's fine,' Merida said. 'I'm a bit of a leaky tap at the moment.'

'You're allowed to be. I hear that I'm going to have to stick around for a while longer if I want to know whether I have a granddaughter or a grandson.'

'You will.' Merida gave a small laugh as he put her at ease over the painful topic of his health.

'You're not going to find out before?'

'I didn't plan to.' And then she wondered if per-haps she should. And then, although it should be Ethan she first told about the baby moving, she chose not to keep this moment from Jobe. 'I just felt the baby move for the first time.'

'Seriously?'

Merida nodded.

'Then the baby must approve of the marriage,'

Jobe said. 'I know that I do.' He gave her a smile. 'Are you ready to come and have a seat inside?'

She nodded.

'I don't know about you, but I sure as hell need one.'

Merida had never expected to find one tonight, but she felt as if she had a friend.

An unlikely one.

'What were you and my father talking about?' Ethan asked when she joined him again at the pretty round table. 'I told him not to talk about the share-holders' meeting tonight...'

'He was telling me that he used to bring you here,' Merida said. 'And I told him that I'd just felt the baby move.'

'You felt it move?'

Merida nodded and she watched a rare smile stretch his lips. 'He asked if we were going to find out what we're having.'

'And are we?' Ethan asked, his face moving in close.

'I don't know,' Merida said.

And then she was feeling the graze of his lips on hers, and she simply forgot where they were as they shared in a soft tender kiss.

Glasses clinked as they were hit with knives, and the guests at the table called for more. Merida blinked and pulled back. The taste of him was still on her lips and the flush in her cheeks was real.

She caught Jobe's eye and saw him smiling, and—stupid her—she started to believe there might really be hope for them. It was a beautiful wedding.

Eventually they headed for another photo opportunity to the decking outside, with the skyline stunning behind them.

Ethan kissed her again there—for the cameras, of course.

And, had he loved her, then it really would have been the perfect wedding. Because just as Merida started flagging, as the faces she had only just started to put names to started blurring, Ethan put an arm around her.

'Let's get you home.'

They left their own celebration early, though word had got out as to where they were, so there were the inevitable cameras waiting for them—but so too was the car.

Back over the bridge they went, and Merida felt spun into a world where she didn't belong, but wanted to.

The lights and the shadows from the bridge had a strobe effect on her face, and Ethan was shocked into realising that he cared for her more than he should.

But he didn't *know* her.

The only thing he actually knew was that she would leave.

He didn't know where that had come from, but he felt as if it was carved on the steel wall surrounding his heart—one day she would simply be gone.

And he was prepared for that. He had all the 'i's dotted and the 't's crossed in their contract, because to Ethan it was as inevitable as that.

* * *

Her first glimpse of his home brought actual tears to her eyes.

It wasn't the sight of the gorgeous building that blew her away, but the trees outside, which had been decorated with fairy lights, and the fact that there were gardenias around the doorway.

'Ethan...' She could not think of anything more welcoming.

They were away from the celebrations now. The toasts had been made, the photographers and cameramen had packed up and gone, and now, close to midnight, it was just them.

And he'd done this.

Well, Merida doubted he'd been wrestling with lights and fuses and flowers, but the fact that he'd arranged it touched her.

Merida climbed out of the car and stood on the street, looking up at the apartment building and just drinking the decorations in.

'It's beautiful,' Merida said. 'Seriously...'

Merida didn't get to finish. Ethan scooped her up into his arms.

'And so are you.'

'Stop it!' She was laughing, kicking. She had never imagined him like this—or maybe she had, and now she felt that, even for a very hasty wedding, they'd somehow got it right.

The doorman held open the door as Ethan carried her over the threshold and kissed her so hard that her arms went to his neck.

Oh, would he ever *not* turn her on? Merida wondered.

She had ached for them to be alone—to talk, to make sense of the million details and plans—but now she simply drowned in his kiss. And he kissed her all the way to the elevator, so she was burning in his arms as he carried her inside.

The doors slid closed and the elevator jolted. So too did her heart.

'Okay…' he stopped kissing her and carefully put her down.

Merida was disorientated, slightly giddy, and in unfamiliar surroundings with a now unfamiliar man—for gone was the passion of before.

'You can stop acting now,' he said.

CHAPTER TWELVE

ETHAN'S WORDS PLAYED on repeat as they stepped out at the penthouse floor.

'You can stop acting now.'

For a while she had forgotten that this was a contracted wedding—an marriage of utter convenience and a staged event. Certainly as he'd kissed her all the way through the door the fact that there might be cameras trained on them had been the furthest thing from her mind.

Ethan seemed oblivious to the brutal slap his words had delivered—although perhaps not quite, because he frowned when he saw her pale lips.

'Bed,' he said. 'You look wiped.'

The apartment was on two levels, but Merida barely took it in. She simply felt numb as she followed him up the staircase. The master suite seemed to take up the entire top floor. The curtains were drawn and the furnishings were rich and heavy. There was a very masculine feel to the room.

'You have a beautiful home,' Merida said, but she was making small talk and not quite ready for that huge bed.

'I have a beautiful wife,' Ethan responded, and dropped his jacket onto a chair.

'I thought we'd stopped acting?' Merida snapped out a tart response, but better that than reveal how raw his words had left her.

'We have. I'm just stating a truth.'

He removed his tie, and Merida watched as he easily dealt with his shoes and socks. Next came his shirt. And his eyes never left her face.

'I think it all went well,' Ethan said.

'Was I convincing enough for you?' She flashed angry eyes but he wasn't perturbed.

In fact he came over to her. 'Very. Here, let me help.'

He easily located the small concealed zip on her dress, and as he pulled it down Merida closed her eyes, because despite herself she craved his touch. She wanted to turn and be in his arms and she was fighting with herself.

Beneath the dress she wore a thin pale gold slip with spaghetti straps, and he helped her out of that and dropped it to the floor.

He saw, for the first time, all the changes in her.

His hand dusted over her stomach for a moment, but then moved lower and slid her knickers down.

Merida stepped out of them on legs that were shaky, grateful for the steadiness of his arm. And when he unhooked her bra she looked down and saw the pink of her areolae and her nipples like two studs, jutting out.

The air crackled between them as he stroked one.

She watched, wondering how, as if with a switch, he simply turned her on.

'Come to bed,' he told her in a low, throaty voice.

And she could blame it on the contract, on the fact that a marriage had to be consummated, but as she climbed in Merida went because she *needed* to.

He discarded his trousers and she looked at that gorgeous body naked. Pale and long-limbed, he was also toned and lithe—and already hard. He climbed into bed and there was no chatter, no speaking, just the heat of his naked body as he pulled her into him.

And she went to him like an addict, searching for the knock-out effect of his tongue.

He'd expected martyrdom to strike in the marital bed tonight, yet there wasn't a trace of that.

Merida had been on a slow burn all day, with end-less kisses that had clouded her mind, and it was a relief simply to give in to the constant push-pull of desire.

Later she would think, fathom how to proceed, but all Merida knew was that she needed him badly *tonight*.

They were all entwined limbs and searching tongues, and she was ready when he entered her slick warmth.

He took her as he would have the first time, had Merida not told him she was a virgin. Oh, not against the wall… But she was the first woman in this bed and he took her hot and hard against the mattress, wrapping her legs around his loins and driving hard.

CHAPTER THIRTEEN

MERIDA AWOKE IN a vast empty bed.

Today their brief honeymoon ended and Ethan returned to work. They hadn't really left the bed, apart from brief trips to the fridge or to shower or bathe together.

It was just after six in the morning and there was a feeling of decadence in her even before she opened her eyes. There were rings on her finger and between her legs she was tender and she was Ethan Devereux's wife.

And a mother-to-be.

She lay on her back, and that flutter she had felt on her wedding day was back. Her hand cupped her stomach, but there was nothing she could feel with her hand.

Unsure of what to do, Merida got out of bed. On the rare occasions she'd half dressed over the past day or so, it had been in his shirts. Her wedding dress still lay on the floor, but she rescued the pale silk slip she had worn beneath and put it on.

This was home.

Not that she knew the address.

Merida wandered around.

The view was stunning. From every window there was a picture-postcard view of Manhattan but she had no real idea of where she was.

Ethan disorientated her.

Not deliberately—she got that. But from the day they had met he had upended her world like a snow globe and she kept waiting for the glitter to settle.

She came to the kitchen, which looked like something from a magazine—all gleaming appliances and in the centre a huge black wood table.

It was as male as a kitchen could be.

She opened up the fridge. There were some of the platters he'd had sent in from Barnaby's that they had made good inroads into, and there was a carton of juice and some milk.

She poured some juice and then settled down to read the huge influx of messages on her phone, from friends clearly surprised by the wedding.

And not just old ones.

Reece was suddenly terribly gushing, and even Anton, who'd been furious with her when she'd left the show, had sent his congratulations and a cryptic message.

I get it now.

Merida frowned, not really understanding, but then it dawned on her—Anton now understood why she was keeping the baby. Because it was Ethan Devereux's.

It rattled her, and Merida swiftly swiped to the next message.

It was from Naomi, asking that she call her, and adding, I hope the press hasn't upset you too much.

And so, of course, Merida went straight to the news.

They'd avoided all that yesterday, and simply spent the day in bed, but today the real world was creeping in.

Devereux Gold!

She looked at a picture of herself and Ethan on the court house steps and read the little caption about the bride wearing gold and how much the colour suited her.

It wasn't actually said, but the implication was clear. They were calling her a gold-digger.

She read on a little, about her 'failed acting career', and wanted to dispute what was said. But there was nowhere for her to do so, and she clicked to the next headline.

A Very Sudden Wedding

In this picture the wind had caught at her dress, and for all the world to see there was the visible reason for their marriage.

'Ignore them.'

She looked up and there was Ethan. He was wearing grey track pants and a grey top and was breathless. And in that moment she learned two new things about her new husband.

That he ran in the morning before he went to work. And that he looked gorgeous even sweaty and dishevelled.

'They've painted me as a gold-digger,' Merida said.

'Oh, well.' He shrugged, and then opened his mouth to make a flip comment about occasionally the press getting things right. But perhaps wisely he chose not to exercise his black humour.

'Is that all you have to say?'

'Merida.' Annoyingly calm, he responded, 'If I have to give my in-depth thoughts on every headline I appear in then we're in for some long breakfasts.'

'They're saying that I'm pregnant.'

'Well, you *are*.' He shrugged again.

'Our child might one day read this,' Merida said. 'They're insinuating that you married me because of the baby...' Her breath caught—because, well, he *had*—but she pushed on. 'And that I'm nothing more than a gold-digger and a failed actress. Where did they *get* that?'

'I have no idea,' Ethan said. 'Though I *shall* have a word with Howard. He should have known better than to put you in a gold dress. A five-year-old could have seen where that would lead.'

And that, according to Ethan, was the end of that, only it wasn't enough for Merida.

'Do *you* think I'm a gold-digger, Ethan?'

She was brave enough to ask it outright, and when their eyes met he gave her a very honest answer.

'I don't care.'

He didn't.

The 'i's were dotted the 't's were crossed and to Ethan the whys and wherefores just didn't matter, because right now they could simply enjoy it all.

And he *did* enjoy her.

All of her.

He'd thought their marriage would be a disaster, but two days in he was coming around.

Not only was the sex brilliant, but he liked their conversations. The way she challenged his assumptions, the way she had popped into his head mid-run and he'd raced to get back.

There was a connection—he could feel it—and he'd never really known that before.

'Come on,' he said, assuming the conversation was over. 'I'll show you around before I get ready.'

'I've had a look,' Merida said, but she knew she was being a misery and so she stood. 'I ought to tidy up…'

'Don't be ridiculous. Rita will be in today. I suddenly thought, when I was running,' Ethan said as they headed out of the kitchen, 'that if something happened to you, you wouldn't be able to give your address.' He told her, 'You're just around the corner from your old workplace and a couple of blocks down from Jobe.'

'Do you see him much?'

'Every day at work,' Ethan said as he showed her around. 'Don't worry, he won't be dropping round…'

'I don't mind,' Merida said. 'I like him.'

The lower floor of the apartment contained a large south-facing lounge and it was Merida's favourite, with jade curtains and gorgeous dark silk rugs and walls. The area was vast enough to easily carry it off. There was also a large dining room, with a gleaming table, and a library, as well as an office and two guest bedrooms.

They walked back up to the master suite. 'Call Howard,' Ethan said. 'I've told him to expect you. He can help you with clothes and things.'

'Clothes?'

'You arrived with *one* suitcase,' Ethan pointed out, just as Merida found out that the master suite didn't actually take up the entire top floor. Down the long hallway they came to a double door that Merida hadn't seen before.

Behind it was a small set of stairs, which they climbed. They came to a large empty room, with skylights, and Merida looked around and admired the stunning space.

Ethan admired her.

The sun streaming in caught her hair, and she was clearly naked beneath the sheer slip.

'It's gorgeous, Ethan,' Merida said. 'How come it's empty?'

'I never quite knew what to do with it,' he admitted. 'I was thinking that the nanny and the baby can go up here.'

'The nanny?'

'Of course.'

'Ethan, there's no need for a nanny—'

'Merida,' he cut it. 'When I'm not in the Middle East I have commitments four or five evenings a week. For at least half of them you'll be expected to join me. And you'll have lunches and functions to attend. Not too many at first, but the Devereux family supports a lot of arts and various charities. You'll need a nanny. And,' he added, 'once you're gone so shall I.'

He just dropped the fact that their marriage was temporary into the conversation as easily as that. As if she was a weather front passing through, strewing babies in her wake and then rolling on.

'There's more than enough room for a nanny and the baby up here,' Ethan said, 'as well as a decent-sized playroom. But I'll leave it to you. And don't worry,' he added. 'I shan't be making the same mistake as my father.'

For the first time he addressed extensive rumours.

'Nannies really aren't my thing.'

His words were flippant and light, but Merida could see the tension in his jaw, and there was a flicker of muscle in his cheek.

'Are you ever going to forgive him?' Merida asked. 'Ethan, it was years ago.'

'Yes, my mother's been in the ground for *twenty-five* years, to be precise.'

He would say no more than that on the subject, and turned the conversation back to the space in which they stood, waving a dismissive hand at the skylights. 'Just enjoy yourself with it.'

'What? Decorating your apartment and hiring your nanny?'

He didn't react to her sarcasm. Instead he headed back down the stairs.

'I'll get some designers in,' he said. 'Whatever you think will work.'

They were back in the kitchen now, and he looked at her, at her knot of hair and at that slip that clung to her body. He walked over and held her by the arms, and for the second time in his life—and it only happened when Merida was present—he was tempted not to go to work.

Merida looked at Ethan as he held her, and she could feel the shift—not only in him but in her. She was so easily turned on by his gaze.

'I've got to get ready,' he told her, and Merida nodded.

His eyes asked if she was coming upstairs to join him in the shower, but Merida declined with two words. 'Then go.'

She was hurting, bruised by his reference to her leaving and the fact that he simply didn't care if she was here for the money or not.

Yet his dirty kiss and primed body turned her to liquid and, pressed against the bench, she was putty in his skilled hands.

He was so rangy and potent—so ready at any given moment to take her.

'Come on, Merida…' he said, his hand gliding between her thighs to where she was warm and damp.

'You've got to get ready.'

She didn't shove him off, just gave a slight push to his chest, but it was contrary to all the time they had spent together so far.

There was a slight narrowing of his eyes as he tried to interpret this shift in her, but he soon headed up the stairs and descended only a short while later.

He looked exquisite, Merida thought as she stood, leaning against the bench, nursing a coffee she had made.

His hair was damp, but fell into perfect shape, and he was clean-shaven and wearing a hefty dose of that gorgeous cologne.

He cursed as he read his phone. 'I've got to go.'

He was back to being the businessman she had first met, but he removed her coffee from her to give her a kiss and a decent squeeze of her bottom, which rather told her that he would take up from where they had left off when he got home later.

'Don't go getting dressed, now,' Ethan said with a light tease, but he did not see the dangerous glint in Merida's eyes.

She heard the door close and finally, after the shock of his proposal, their whirlwind wedding and two days spent in bed, the glitter seemed to settle and Merida took in her surroundings.

She stood in a loveless marriage.

Well, not loveless. She was crazy about Ethan. If

there was such a thing as love at first sight, then that was what had happened to her.

Except he didn't want a bar of it.

She could not spend a year on call to him. Could not keep giving herself to him over and over, with no reward for her heart.

A loveless marriage could only work, Merida decided, if there was *no* love on either side. But a regular dose of unrequited love might very nearly kill her.

It was making love to her, and just sex to him.

Never mind the turmoil she felt, or her feelings for him, to Ethan this was no more than a business transaction with sex thrown in.

But no more.

Their earlier conversation wasn't over.

If Ethan thought he had a gold-digger for a wife, then she would *act* like one.

Merida was new to all this, so she did a quick tidy-up before Rita arrived, then showered and looked at the few clothes she had with her.

She would need a lot more than her lucky kilt to survive this.

Merida called Howard and got to work. Or rather, the work of being a Devereux wife.

Ethan came home at seven to a gorgeous wife—though he rather missed the curls. She was dressed in a simple grey shift and there was the scent of beef bourguignon from Barnaby's wafting through the stunning apartment.

The table was set and they took their seats.

'Anton Del Bosco got in touch,' Ethan said. 'It was noted that I'd left during the first half of *Night Forest* and he's invited us both to attend another performance.'

'No, thank you.'

'We *have* to do this sort of thing, Merida,' Ethan stated.

'Well, I'd prefer not to go and see the show I had to bow out of,' Merida said. 'How was the rest of your day?'

'Long,' he admitted. 'I need a *very* early night.'

Merida nodded. 'Well, I shan't be disturbing you— I've moved my things into the front guest room.'

'The front guest room?'

'It's a bit bigger than the other one, and I like—'

'What the hell are you going on about?' Ethan interrupted.

'I think we should have separate rooms.'

He must have thought she was joking, because for a moment he smiled.

'I'm serious, Ethan. I'll tell Rita that the front guest room is being refurbished and keep it locked when she's here.'

Merida had thought it all through. She simply could not give of herself—give her heart—night after night after night, to a man who thought so little of her. She could not count down the days until it was all over.

'The marriage is consummated,' Merida told him, and went on with what she had decided. 'I'll attend all the necessary functions, and I'll sort out the nanny's area and the nursery, and have everything running smoothly for the baby before I'm gone.'

Merida would take her role seriously. She would be the perfect Devereux wife. But she would never for a moment forget the reason she was here.

She carried Devereux property.

That was it.

'I'll do everything that's stated in the contract, and everything that you pay me to do I'll do well, but I won't be your whore for a year,' Merida said.

She put down her knife and fork and excused herself from the table.

'We sleep separately from now on.'

CHAPTER FOURTEEN

MERIDA PERFORMED BEAUTIFULLY in her new role.

If there was ever to be an award for Contracted Wives then it would go to Ms Merida Cartwright—which was now her defunct stage name.

She and Ethan were seen out, holding hands at intimate dinners, Merida elegant and coiffed as she gazed adoringly into his eyes. They attended formal functions with Merida blending in accordingly. Her growing bump was perfectly dressed in shades of black, powder-blue and silver-grey, and she had a whole row of various shades of neutral shoes.

'Let the eyes fall on the diamonds.' That was Howard's favourite tip, and Merida always smiled when he said that and thanked him.

She did, however, resist Howard's strong suggestion that she get foils to tame her red mane at least down to a strawberry blonde. But she had a blow dry on alternate days and her hair was always sleek and smooth.

And Ethan was the perfect gentleman.

Well, he was a rather sullen perfect gentleman.

But he'd gone into this with very low expectations of marriage and theirs didn't disappoint.

He felt he understood now the concept of the 'honeymoon period', because for all of two days it had been bliss.

But it was a marriage of convenience, and if sex wasn't on her agenda then his wrist would just have to suffice.

He was way too suave to cajole her.

And as for Merida…?

She tended to sleep in on weekday mornings. It possibly wasn't very wifely, but he was off and running around six, then out through the door just after seven—and she *was* seven months pregnant, after all.

As for the renovations… Who knew? But Merida found she had a hidden skill and was utterly *brilliant* at spending Ethan's money.

'They're going to take out the floor and the stairs,' Merida explained one evening as they headed to his father's. 'And the wall on…' She hesitated, mindful of the driver.

Neither of them wanted it getting out that they slept in separate rooms.

Rita the housekeeper no doubt knew, but Ethan paid enough for her discretion.

'The wall on our floor needs to be moved.'

'Lucky we kept the hotel suite, then,' Ethan said, thinking back to his bachelor days—or rather the night they had spent there.

'There's no need for us to move out,' Merida said

rather hurriedly, because there was only one bedroom in his suite at the hotel.

'Absolutely there is. There's no way that I'm staying in the apartment while there's building going on.'

God, Ethan thought, she really couldn't stand the thought of being in the same bed as him.

'I'll have the couch,' he mouthed, and smiled the dark smile he had invented for her and used a lot of late. And then spoke one word, laced with bitterness. 'Darling.'

Merida breathed deeply and looked out of the window, barely seeing the blazing trees that looked set on fire by autumn—or 'fall', as he called it.

It was a short drive—just two blocks to his father's—but there was no question of their walking. They were dressed for a photo shoot and Ethan was tense.

'I hate these things,' he said, running a finger along the neck of his shirt. 'It shouldn't take too long. It's just a magazine piece. But there'll be some questions.'

'I'll be fine.'

Merida wasn't looking forward to the photo shoot either. Yet she understood that Jobe wanted some pictures with his son and his new wife. She just wished it wasn't all so formal and staged.

But there wasn't time to change the world.

In fact, Jobe didn't have much time at all. He was going into hospital next week, to start a new treatment, but he was fading before their eyes.

Jobe hadn't made it to the annual shareholders' meeting, and he had stepped down a week prior.

'Thank God for the little one,' Jobe had said, because the news that Ethan had married, and that there was a baby on the way, had buoyed things up enough that when their founder stepped down, the shareholders' long-anticipated bloodbath was more of a hiccough.

'I think it's more to do with the Dubai announcement than the baby,' Merida had suggested.

'Well, we're going to have to agree to disagree,' Jobe had said, and smiled.

Jobe and Ethan had said the same thing to Merida on the night they had met. The two men were so alike. And yet, apart from about work, father and son barely spoke.

Time was running out, Merida knew. Not just for Jobe, but for Ethan to build bridges with his father.

If it were even possible.

Once at the stunning Fifth Avenue residence, they were informed that Jobe was getting ready and would be down soon. Ethan and Merida walked into the drawing room.

Abe and Candice were already there. Abe was standing with one elbow on the mantel, nursing a whisky.

'Merida.'

He gave her a nod. They didn't bother with the kiss-kiss thing, and Candice barely looked over.

Ethan and Abe bitched about their good friends Nikkei and Dow Jones as the photographer and interviewer arrived, and as they set up Merida wandered out into the hall and stood looking at family photos of old.

God, Elizabeth had been beautiful, Merida thought as she examined one of the photos.

The stunning family sat on a pale sofa with carefully arranged pastel silk cushions. Elizabeth was holding the newborn Ethan. Her long blond hair was brushed so that it fell over her left shoulder and she held Ethan on her right. Jobe sat beside her, with a serious-looking Abe on his knee.

'Merida!'

She turned and smiled at the sound of her name. At least Jobe seemed pleased to see her.

He made his way rather slowly down the stairs, and gave her a kiss on the cheek.

'Tell me, Jobe,' Merida said, and smiled. 'Do these photos get taken down when you have a new wife in residence?'

Jobe laughed. 'Nope—she's the boys' mother.'

'Boys?' Merida raised a questioning eyebrow.

'They always will be boys to me. You just wait till you have your own.'

Merida smiled. She thought of her own parents, barely in touch, and doubted there were *any* family pictures of her own childhood lining their walls.

'You're a good dad, Jobe.'

'I wanted to be.'

It was an odd answer, and she heard his pensive tone, but now he was walking ahead of her and into the drawing room.

Merida was interviewed as the photographer did some test shots.

'Merida, you were working at a gallery when you and Ethan met?'

'Yes.' She smiled.

'And did Ethan drop in often?'

'He did.' She smiled again. 'There was a gorgeous amulet display, owned by Sheikh Prince Khalid…'

Merida was faultless in her responses, Ethan thought. And when they did a couple of headshots of her he watched her laugh and smile. She was just so relaxed and at ease with it all.

Ethan missed the old them.

And not just the sex.

While their time together before the news of the baby had been short-lived, he missed the walking through the city, the coffee and the sharing.

And in that brief time just after their marriage—well, he'd felt as if he might take on the world.

Now, from where he stood, Merida had got what she wanted. The marriage was consummated, her duty was done and now they awaited the baby, followed by an amicable divorce.

The photos took for ever, but finally it was over. Abe and Candice were gone before the photographer's bags were even packed, and it was Ethan who saw then off.

The interviewer was still gushing. 'We'd love to come and see your home when the renovations are complete—and of course once the baby arrives…'

Ethan said nothing. He was going along with it

for now, but there was no way he was having them in his home. No way he would subject his child…

His child.

Their child.

He closed the door and as he did so the photos lining the walls seemed to taunt him.

God, he loathed being here, because the creeping of the past tightened like a vine.

He remembered now the summons to perfection. His nails being cut, the clip-clip-clip and the rake of a comb through his hair.

'Ethan, smile…' his mother would croon in unfamiliar affectionate tones as they sat perfectly on the pale blue sofa. 'Come on, darling.'

And then, as he stood there in the vast hallway, he remembered another day. A morning.

Meghan, his nanny, was shouting as she carried him through the house. 'You left him in the car!'

Ethan remembered being hauled out of a car and stripped off, and the coolness of a shower and water being poured down his throat.

'He was asleep!' His mother had been shouting too. 'It seemed mean to wake him.'

He hadn't understood why Meghan had been crying. Why Meghan had said sorry to him, over and over, as she cooled him down, when it hadn't been her fault.

Ethan was sweating as much as if he'd been running. He pressed the bridge of his nose between finger and thumb and screwed closed his eyes, willing the memory to be gone.

He wanted to go back to normality. Or the strange version of it he and Merida now made.

Ethan pushed open the drawing room door and it was clear that he had interrupted a conversation.

'Everything okay?' Jobe checked, because his son was ghostly white.

'Everything's fine. What are you two up to?'

'I was just saying to Merida—why on earth would you move into a hotel when you could come here…?'

'I left home nearly twenty years ago,' Ethan snapped. 'I've no intention—'

'Ethan,' Jobe interrupted. 'I'm spending more time at the hospital than here. There's a full staff. I don't like the thought of the place standing empty, and there's no need for your pregnant wife to be staying in a hotel. However luxurious, it's not a home.'

Had his father not been dying, Ethan would have told him in no uncertain terms what he could do with that idea, but he saved his verdict for after their car ride home.

'No way.'

'Well, *I* think it's a nice idea.'

'Seriously?' He gaped, and then he looked at her. 'Whatever, Merida—it makes no difference to me.'

'Meaning…?'

'I'm heading to the Middle East tomorrow.'

'For how long?'

'Four weeks.' He plucked a figure from his head.

'Your father's *dying*, Ethan, and you're heading off for a month?'

'Yes,' Ethan said. 'He's the one who wants the ball to keep rolling—well, hotels don't build themselves.'

Yes, he was running away. But there was no way he was staying in that house. As well as that, he was sick of this farcical marriage, with the stilted dinners and the strained nights out when they smiled, again and again, for the cameras. When they kissed and held hands in the hope that someone was watching, then dropped all contact the moment they were home.

It was killing him, lying upstairs night after night while she slept in the guest room.

'We couldn't sleep separately at my father's…' Ethan said, and watched her rapid blink.

'Rita knows…'

'Rita was born before sex was invented,' Ethan quipped. 'She thinks it's normal for married couples to sleep apart. My father has a fleet of staff…'

Ethan actually no longer gave a damn what the staff thought. It was more a matter of his own wounded pride and, though he loathed their sleeping arrangements, the thought of them lying together night after night and not touching was just impossible.

'You're the one who wanted separate rooms, Merida. Well, I'm going to give you a whole lot more—separate countries. Is that enough space for you?'

CHAPTER FIFTEEN

MERIDA LIKED VISITING JOBE. He was having another round of treatment in the hope of still being around when his grandchild arrived.

'How are you?' She gave him a kiss on the cheek.

'Tired,' Jobe admitted.

'Ethan's calling this evening,' Merida said. 'He wants to know…'

'I just spoke to him online,' Jobe said. 'He told me the ultrasound went well.'

'Yes.'

'Do you know what you're having?'

'No.' She shook her head, and then looked at Jobe and the grey tinge to his skin. 'I could ask my OB to come and speak to you, tell you…'

'You'd do that for me?'

'Of course I would.' Merida smiled, but tears were threatening as they both silently admitted that there might not the time to find out. She set about examining his flowers, rather than let Jobe see the glint of tears.

'These are gorgeous,' she said, burying her face

in a huge bunch of red roses and having a sneaky
read of the card.

'Who's Chantelle?'

'An ex.'

'She doesn't sound as if she wants to be an ex,'
Merida said. 'It says here that she's "desperate to
see you".'

If it had been one of the boys reading his cards
Jobe would have snapped at him, but he liked Me-
rida. And he wanted her for his son. He wanted a
Devereux marriage to finally work.

And so he told Merida, when he'd told no one
else, why he'd ended things with Chantelle. 'I don't
want any spectators.'

'Is that what I am?' Merida checked.

'Yes, but you're family.'

And that made her want to cry too.

He called her over, and Merida sat on the bed and
held his hand.

'I worry about the boys. Less about Ethan, now
that he has you.'

Merida squeezed his hand. At the wedding she'd
been certain Jobe knew it was all a farce. He probably did, she decided. But maybe it was easier for
him to think that his youngest son had settled down.

She doubted it was true.

It had been months since the wedding, and it terrified her to think what Ethan might be getting up
to in Dubai. She wondered if that was why he'd gone
there…

Marriage to a Devereux, Merida had long-ago decided, was hard work indeed.

'Do you miss Elizabeth?' Merida asked, inviting him to talk about his late wife, the mother of his sons.

'Not for a moment,' Jobe said, and Merida swallowed at this unexpected response.

'You were happy, though…'

And maybe it was the morphine speaking, or perhaps it was after decades of hurt as he moved to the end of his life, but for once Jobe did not keep everything in.

'Marriage to Elizabeth was the most hellish time of my life,' Jobe said.

Merida was stunned. 'But you've got pictures of her everywhere…you speak so nicely of her…'

'Well, you don't speak ill of the dead, do you?' He shook his head. 'It's easier for the boys—to let them think that she loved them…'

'She *didn't* love them?'

'The only person Elizabeth ever loved,' Jobe said, 'was herself.'

And then he told her something else. A truth. One so vital that Ethan and Abe must surely be told.

But Jobe refused. 'I'm taking that to the grave.'

'Jobe, no.'

It was a revelation. And Merida truly didn't know what it meant, or what to do with it. Or even if she should do anything.

Ethan was so closed off on the rare times that he called. And to keep up the façade Merida was terminally brittle.

Yet she ached for him, for more information, and as she let herself into the house after her visit she lay drained on the bed and admitted the truth.

The Devereux family was the family she had never had.

Oh, they were messed up, but they'd all been there at her wedding. Jobe checked in on the welfare of their baby all the time, and Ethan, the husband who didn't love her, still had the ability to melt her heart.

Even on a computer screen.

Tonight he was wearing, of all things, a robe and *keffiyeh*.

'Don't ask,' he said by way of greeting. 'I've been calling you.'

Merida stared at her screen and magnified his impossibly beautiful face. 'I've been busy.'

'Too busy to pick up your phone?'

'Yes,' she said.

It was true—she had been too busy crying, and the very last thing she wanted to give him was a glimpse of her tears.

Playing the part of a cold-hearted gold-digger was far easier than showing him her heart.

'How's Dubai?'

'Hot,' he said.

Hell, he thought.

His playboy days were over. And as he stared at his bride he thought, Who would ever imagine they slept in separate rooms?

'I'm about to head out for dinner with Khalid, but I wanted to speak to you first.'

'Regarding…?'

She sounded like his PA, Ethan thought.

'I wanted to know if you'd had any luck finding a nanny.'

'Not yet,' Merida admitted. 'Ethan, do you remember I told you my friend was a maternity nanny?'

He nodded without thinking, because he remembered every minute of every hour of that time when they had been close. And they'd been so close that morning—lying in bed, talking and laughing with what had felt like the world waiting for them.

'Well,' Merida continued, 'I was thinking of asking her to be here for the first few weeks.'

'Am I running an English backpackers' hostel?'

She never knew if he was joking.

'Fine,' he said when she didn't smile. 'If it makes it easier on you.'

Merida hoped it would.

'But you do need to find a permanent nanny.'

'I'm trying, but they're all so very formal…'

He nodded. 'Tell me about it.'

'Were they awful?' Merida asked. 'The nannies you had?'

'Not awful—they were just very strict. Meghan, the one I had when I was young…' He hesitated. 'Well, she was nice, from what I can remember. But we all know how *that* worked out.'

'I don't,' Merida said, and stared back at him. 'All I know is the salacious stuff that I've read in the newspapers.'

'That's all I know too,' Ethan said. 'She was nice. Clearly my father thought so too.' And then he admitted something. 'I missed Meghan dreadfully when she was gone.'

Merida stared harder. It was the first honest conversation they had had in months, and his first real revelation about that time.

And while they were speaking—really speaking—there was something she needed to say.

'Ethan...' She was hesitant to push. After all, it wasn't her place—she was a contract wife only. Yet, whether or not he wanted it, she was more than that in her heart. 'Your father doesn't look well. I think you need to come home.'

'Someone has to work. I speak to him online every day, and he's repeatedly said that he wants business as usual.'

'It's not the same as seeing face to face.'

No, it wasn't.

He could see Merida, and he could hear her. But it wasn't the same as being there.

'You and your father need to sort things out while you still can.'

'Just leave it, Merida.'

She'd pushed it too far, Merida knew. And so she clipped on her mask and fixed him with cold green eyes that were iced by unshed tears.

'Fine.' She gave him a tight smile. 'Now I really do have to go.'

'Not yet...'

As strained as they were, speaking with Merida

was the highlight of his day. And so he tried to prolong things in a way that usually worked.

'There are some amazing jewellers here. How
about—?'

'Ethan!' Merida snapped. She didn't want him
coming home bearing gifts. She just wanted him
home. Only she dared not admit that. 'I need to go.'

God, but she was brittle, Ethan thought, and then
cancelled dinner.

What the hell had happened to the gorgeous red-
head he'd met? The one who had somehow made
him smile?

She'd turned into Candice, Ethan thought. Bought
and paid for and barely scraping through the small
talk.

Yet they *had* spoken.

'I think you need to come home.'

The words gnawed at him, for Ethan knew that
was where he ought to be. But he'd tried to speak to
his father just this morning, and all Jobe had wanted
to talk about was the new hotel complex, and how
he agreed with Ethan that he wanted the Devereux
name in Al-Zahan. They spoke about *nothing* else.

He got undressed and lay on the bed, staring
blindly while thinking of home.

He was starting to remember things. Ethan was
starting to remember things about his mother that
made all he'd believed a lie.

Yes, she had been beautiful and everything he'd
read said that she'd been kind, and the photos in his
father's house told the tale of a wonderful childhood.

But they were just paper pictures, hung on walls, and empty words had shaped his perceptions.

And then he heard a voice, its husk a familiar one, and it had him turning his attention to the entertainment screen.

Merida.

In one of her many guises. But there she was. Walking over Gapstow Bridge, clipping along in high heels, one so worn that its metal spike hit the ground with each step of her right foot.

He almost didn't recognise her.

Oh, physically he did, of course—there was the blaze of her red hair and her gorgeous green eyes— but she looked jaded, bitter, as if all the light had died in her eyes.

Merida looked the part she played—a tired, world-weary cheap hooker.

He flicked the switch and watched her walk backwards, then played the scene over and over again.

She was a brilliant actress. He'd never actually seen her perform, but now, as he watched and rewatched the scene over and over, Ethan felt as if he'd been given some key information.

He recalled all their conversations, and he remembered her on their wedding day, in the back of the car, and what she had said about her parents and not wanting to let them know they'd hurt her.

Was that what she was doing with him?

Hiding her pain behind a perfect mask?

Making out she was a gold-digger when she might just have loved him all along?

He reached for his tablet and pulled up the photos that the magazine had sent through.

He looked at her smile and zoomed right in.

Merida really was a brilliant actress. Not even the most diligent viewer would be able to see that her smile didn't reach her eyes.

Even he had to flick through them all and then compare them to the images in his mind of the *real* Merida. The one he had seen on the night they met and the morning he had said goodbye. Merida *before* the baby and the end of her career and the gold-digging accusations and the contract.

He wanted to meet her again.

But there were walls of ice between them—the contract, the harsh words, and now Merida was playing the part of the society wife.

Ethan wanted to get behind the mask.

If Merida would give him a second chance.

CHAPTER SIXTEEN

His plane hit the Tarmac at two a.m. Eastern Time. It would be the middle of the morning in Dubai. Ethan had told no one he was coming home.

The code for the door worked and he stepped into the entrance hall.

Even as a young man he had had his own wing here, and rarely crossed paths with his father or whomever he had been seeing at the time.

Abe had moved out at eighteen and Ethan had done the same.

Of course he came back on regular occasions, and many a cocktail party or dinner was held here. Yet he hadn't slept here in years. Hadn't climbed these stairs, lined with picture-perfect memories, in ages.

It felt like a taunt.

He pushed open the door to the bedroom and she stirred and then reached out for the light.

'What are you doing back?'

Merida was startled. She knew she looked terrible. She'd had a bath late last night and fallen asleep crying. She did not want him seeing her like this.

'I thought you weren't due back for another week.'

'I missed my loving wife.'

No doubt she thought he was being sarcastic, but it was, in fact, true. Well, not that she was loving, but he had indeed missed Merida.

Her bump was beneath the covers, very visible now, and her hair was wild and untamed, while her eyes were a little red and wary as he started to undress.

He took off his jacket and dropped it on a chair as she asked the question again.

'Why are you back?'

'Because, believe it or not, I do occasionally listen. You're right—nothing's going to get sorted with me over there.'

'You're here to see your father?'

'Yes.'

Amongst other things. But Ethan wanted to be sure that Merida *wasn't* the cool character she portrayed before he told her that.

He still didn't believe in love, but he was willing to test the waters.

'Your hair looks nice,' he told her.

'I fell asleep with it wet.'

'Well, I prefer it that way.'

'Really? Howard thinks I should go blonde.'

'Sack him,' Ethan said—just like that.

'I thought I had to listen to him?'

'Merida, he's at the top of his game, apparently, but if you don't like what he suggests—hell, tell him who's boss. He's supposed to be making your life easier, not turning you into Candice, Version Two.'

He came and sat on the edge of the bed.

Merida wished that he hadn't.

Not because he felt too close, more because when he was this close it killed her to remain apart from him.

His jacket and shirt were off, his socks and shoes too. And she was very aware that she was naked beneath the sheet, so she moved the conversation to the practical.

'I've told the OB to drop in on your father and let him know what we're having.'

'He might let it slip,' Ethan pointed out. 'He's on quite a cocktail of drugs.'

'Well, if he does let it slip it would hardly be the end of the world. I think it's nice that he's interested.'

'I guess…'

'I think I've found a nanny. I interviewed her this afternoon. She's young, fun…'

Ethan turned and looked at her taut features. 'You really don't have to worry there. History won't be repeating itself. I won't do what my father did.'

She looked right back at him and made herself say it. 'No, history *won't* be repeating itself—because if you do hook up with the nanny then I won't be like your mother and swan off to the Caribbean, leaving my baby behind with the two of you. *You'll* be the one to leave. It says so in the contract.'

Ethan's jaw gritted and he buried his face in his hands.

She watched the zip of muscles close down his back and had to clench her fists just to resist reaching out for him, but her words had clearly sunk in, for he looked around the bedroom and told her something.

'I'm starting to remember things.'

'What things?'

'About my mother.'

'Such as?'

'I don't want to talk about it now.'

He looked over to where she lay, rigid and stretched on her side.

'I'm not going to cheat.'

'You already did, Ethan.'

She stared up at the gorgeous ceiling and told him. 'I saw pictures of you at that gala, with that woman, and in the time we were apart there were plenty more.'

'I never slept with any of them.'

'Liar.'

'No,' he said. 'I don't need to lie.'

He rolled towards her and his hand went to her bump, which had grown impressively in the three weeks he'd been gone.

'It's not twins, is it?'

'God, no. Ethan, I've had two scans.'

'I know, but that amulet I held...'

'You've always told me you're not superstitious.'

'I'm not, usually,' Ethan said, 'but you *did* get pregnant that night.'

Merida gave a low laugh. 'Well, it's not twins.'

They lay there and it was nice—the most parents-to-be-like they had ever been. It was innocent, even, just feeling little kicks in the quiet of the night.

'What did the OB say when you saw him last?'

'That I'm a good size,' Merida said. 'That back pain is normal.'

'You've got back pain?'

'A bit—just in my lower back,' Merida said. 'It might be the baby's heels.'

'It's all your ligaments stretching,' Ethan said. 'In preparation.'

He turned to her and gave a triumphant smile at his new knowledge.

Merida couldn't help but smile back. 'Have you been reading?'

'I have.'

She was inordinately pleased. 'When?'

'Well, given that I'm a married man, I knew I couldn't hit the clubs in Dubai, so I bought a book at the airport.'

'A baby book?'

'A pregnancy book. Scared the life out of me,' he admitted. 'Did you speak to Naomi?'

'Yes, she's coming on the first of December and she'll stay until the end of January.'

'That's good.'

The baby had stopped moving and she removed Ethan's hand.

'Goodnight, Ethan.'

He reached over and turned out the light. She heard the slide of his zip as he kicked off his trousers and got under the covers.

And of all the things she had ever done, this was the hardest, for she felt alone even as she lay by his side.

'I saw you on the television,' Ethan said into the darkness.

Merida rolled onto her side. She didn't reply.

'You were very good.'

And still she did not reply. It was safer to pretend she was asleep.

Ethan *never* cajoled. Yet he could *feel* their mutual need. The air beneath the sheet hummed with want, and the heat between them felt as if it choked him.

They had always worked well in the bedroom.

It had to be a start.

Even if she held her guard in every other area, he knew he could win with this.

Merida screwed her eyes closed as he rolled onto his side.

'Where does your back hurt?' he murmured as he ran a finger the length of her spine.

But it didn't feel remedial in the least. In fact, it made her want to bring up her knees.

'Where?' he demanded, and Merida gave up pretending to be asleep.

'There,' she admitted when his hand moved to her lower spine.

He probed with those long fingers and she lay there, eyes closed, but not relaxed to his touch.

'Does that help?'

'A bit.'

He pressed his fingers harder, and then massaged her with the ball of his palm.

'Does *that* help?'

She could barely breathe enough to answer, so she gave a tense nod and then clamped her jaw closed when his mouth came down on her shoulder.

But she did not tell him to stop.

His breathing was harsh as his other arm hooked under her, and she closed her eyes to the bliss of his hand on her breast, dusting over one aching nipple and then rolling it softly.

She could feel the nudge of his erection.

'Merida…'

His voice was low and she could feel him, primed and male behind her. She turned her face to him and his lips brushed her cheek. The scratch of his jaw had her eyes closing as his hand moved from behind her to her front.

Holding back her want was like trying to hold back the tide, and yet she fought with every fibre in her body—from her hands, which yearned to touch him, to her throat, which closed on a sob because she wanted to scream for his touch.

She just wanted to shed the pretence like a skin, to turn her mouth to his.

'I read something else,' he said, as his hand slid past her bump and down to her heat.

'What?'

'That for some women pregnancy makes them more turned on than they've ever been.'

Merida swallowed as his fingers stroked her intimately. He took her right to the edge, kissing her hard, and brought her to a space where she fought not to scream as he slipped in.

It was a deep, sensual bliss. He stroked her as he rocked inside, and buried his face in her hair, and then he started to thrust harder, and she realised she had almost forgotten the power of him.

How he could take her away from herself to a place where heat was the fire they made.

How he could turn her into a frenzied ball of want even when she loathed what they had become.

And how he knew, absolutely *knew*, as he thrust deep inside her, that she was fighting not to come.

'Merida...' he growled, because he could not hold on.

But she would not let go.

Now he got the martyred sex he had expected on their wedding night—but he would not complete until she did.

He turned her.

As the sun rose over the city behind the curtains he brought her to her knees, and she held onto the bed rail as he took her with aching slowness from behind.

And she sobbed and she moaned and she fought to hold on.

'*Come*, Merida,' he told her. 'You can get back to hating me in the morning.'

She shattered with his permission.

It was as if a volt shot up her spine, and she arched and came so deeply that it was he who moaned at the tight clutch of Merida as he filled her.

And never, not for a moment now, would he doubt their love.

He just had to find a way through to her.

Instead of lying spent in his arms, Merida had climbed from the bed and headed to the shower. Appalled at her own lack of restraint and how she had just shattered to his touch.

She vowed, outside the bedroom, never to let down her guard for a second.

But she'd be a liar if she promised to resist him.

CHAPTER SEVENTEEN

THEY CAME TOGETHER at night. Like a guilty dark secret, behind closed doors, he had her over and over.

And Merida in turn had him.

By day she spent his money and played the part of a gold-digger well. But at night she was on her knees.

Tonight, though, was date night. For appearances' sake.

Their last, because tomorrow Naomi arrived.

Merida stared at her reflection and blew out a breath.

They were going to the theatre, to see a top show that they *had* to go to. Not *Night Forest*, of course— she had put her foot down about that—but she was still nervous about going to the theatre.

It had hurt to give it up.

A lot.

Not that she showed it.

She wore a burnt orange dress that clashed magnificently with her hair, and on her slender legs wore high black boots.

As she headed down the stairs Merida wondered as to Ethan's reaction.

'Ready.'

Ethan turned to where Merida stood on the stairs and thought he had never seen her more beautiful than tonight. She made eight and a half months pregnant look sexy.

'Wow!' Ethan said.

Just that.

'I sacked Howard,' Merida told him.

'Thank God.'

'And I've bought an entire new wardrobe.'

'Good for you.'

He did make her smile. And he knew that when he'd sent her to Howard he had, in his backhanded way, only been trying to help her adjust to a very lavish life.

Rather rarely, it wasn't just bed that was on Ethan's mind tonight. He wanted *Merida*. The real one who still eluded him. Oh, he knew that he'd hurt her badly, but he rather hoped he knew where he might find her...

'There's been a change,' he told her. 'We're going to see *Night Forest*.'

He looked up and her face did not crack, but he saw her swallow in the column of her throat.

'I thought we were going to see...'

'Yes, well, Helene got the tickets messed up. And I've been meaning to go. It didn't look good when I walked out the last time. I said we'd drop in on Jobe on the way there.'

'Fine,' Merida said. 'I'll just get my coat.'

It was snowing heavily outside as the car made its way to the hospital.

Ethan was always tense when they visited his father, but tonight he gave Jobe a smile and told him they were headed off to see *Night Forest*.

'You're finally going to see it?' Jobe gave a weary smile.

'We are.' Merida beamed, even though she was shaking inside. Not just at the prospect of going to the theatre, but because Jobe looked so grey.

Ethan watched as Merida went and sat on the edge of his father's bed. He wondered how she did it—how she could be so comfortable in this room when every fibre in his body was on alert, every bleep of a machine had him jumping on the inside.

Not that he showed it. He was a great actor too.

And maybe Merida wasn't quite so together, because after a couple of moments talking she got up off the bed and started looking at Jobe's flowers.

'These are nice,' Merida said. 'From Chantelle?'

Jobe nodded.

'Let her come and see you, Jobe,' Merida pushed.

'I told you. I don't want spectators.' He turned and looked over to Ethan. 'Have you spoken to Maurice?'

'No.'

'Because I want him to...'

'Dad.' *Dad.* Not Jobe. He looked straight at his father. 'I'm not here to speak about work.'

He didn't know how to say any more than that.

How to fill the silence that followed. Because work was really all he had.

It was Merida who filled it. 'Did my obstetrician ever come and see you?' she checked, because Jobe had made no mention of it, and though the doctor had assured her that he had, she wondered if Jobe had perhaps been medicated at the time and forgotten.

'He did.'

'And?'

'I told him there was no need to tell me what you're having because I intend on sticking around to find out.'

Ethan wasn't so sure. 'I'm coming in to see you again tomorrow,' he said.

'You've got the first-of-the-month board meeting, and…'

Ethan held back the hiss in his teeth and wished his father goodnight.

The theatre was packed but, rather than a box, they went straight to the house seats four rows from the front.

It was so close that Merida felt as if she could very possibly reach out and touch the stage.

'How does it feel to be back?' Ethan asked.

'Fine.' She shrugged. 'I'm looking forward to seeing it.'

But she wasn't. Merida was dreading it, in fact.

It was no longer her picture in the programme. And there was a full cast tonight—no announcements, it was all as it said on the programme.

Merida sat there as the lights dimmed and the

curtain lifted and watched the birds flutter home to roost and the night descend on the beautiful forest.

As it had on her career.

She glanced over to Ethan and saw he was lost to the show, utterly oblivious to the agony in her.

He wasn't.

Ethan felt her scramble for a tissue but he made no move. For, just as he needed to face things with his father—and he would tomorrow—Merida needed to do this.

The production was beautiful, stunning, breath-taking. And she had every right to mourn her absence on this stage. Yet not once had she thrown it back at him, Ethan thought.

Ethan's hand closed over hers, and for a moment Merida clung to his strength and this rare warmth outside of the bedroom.

Ah, but that was right—they were on show now, Merida thought, and pulled her hand away.

But then he pressed a handkerchief into her hand, just as Jobe had done on their wedding day, and he took her hand and held it. As if he would never let it go.

When Belladonna came out and sang her solo, Merida rested her head on his shoulder.

'You'll be back,' he told her quietly.

'I don't think so.'

'I *know* so.'

Ethan did know so—for after the production they would speak. Tomorrow he would speak with his father, but tonight was just for them.

It had to be, for her friend would arrive in the morning and in a couple of weeks the baby would be here.

And so, thinking he was being cruel to be kind, he had brought her here, to reduce her to tears, so he could pick her up and hopefully they could start over again.

But now she was pulling away.

Merida felt a tightening in her stomach and shifted in her seat. She was more than used to them, but unlike the others this seemed to move round to her back.

And then, just as the lights came up for the interval, Merida felt another one.

'You miss it, don't you?' Ethan said, but his voice seemed to be coming from a million miles away.

'Merida?' Ethan said. 'I know that you must miss it, but—'

'My private thoughts are not a part of our contract,' Merida hissed, and her words were far harsher than she had intended, though she did not really know why. 'Even you, with all your millions, can't *afford* to know how I feel.'

'I don't get what you're saying.'

'You can't have it all, Ethan. You can't have every part of me. Because I need something to be left when our time is over...'

She couldn't do this here. They were out in public and starting to row. The façade was slipping, the mask falling down, and she sat there on a red velvet seat and scrambled to find the Merida she had created. The tough persona, the perfect wife...

She felt adrift on turbulent waters, with nothing to cling to.

'I'm fine,' Merida said suddenly, and she looked at his black eyes, narrowed in concern.

But her back was really hurting, and she couldn't stand to sit through the second half. She just wanted to be alone.

Merida just wanted to be away from here.

'Excuse me,' she said.

She wasn't going to the restroom, although naturally that was what Ethan assumed. Instead she walked past the chattering, laughing people and then squeezed through the thick throng of patrons who were all heading back in as she made her way outside.

It was as light as if it was daytime, and she stood there for a moment, unsure as to how she even felt, let alone what she should do.

'Merida...'

She turned to the sound of his voice.

'Just go back in,' she sobbed, and now she was really starting to cry.

'Merida,' He was as calm and as unruffled as only he could be. 'Are you in labour?'

'I can't be!' she cried. 'I don't want the baby to come now.'

'I don't think you get to decide,' Ethan said calmly. 'Why not now?'

'Because we're not ready.'

He could have been facetious and said they had a nanny arriving tomorrow, a driver waiting and the renovations were almost done, but there were times when he had to be serious.

'We will be,' Ethan said, and he took her in his arms and steadied her. 'I promise you that.'

CHAPTER EIGHTEEN

IT WAS THE strangest feeling to have a father in one part of the hospital, close to the end of his life. And a future life in another.

'We're not ready,' Merida kept saying.

'Well, according to your obstetrician, we've got ages,' Ethan said, but it probably wasn't the time to be making jokes about the fact that she was only three centimetres dilated.

It was suggested that Merida try and have a sleep before the hard work of pushing began.

'Merida,' Ethan said. 'We *are* ready. I've been doing an awful lot of thinking and—'

'I can't do this now,' Merida said.

She knew she was close to the edge, and that any minute now she would break down and confess just how much she loved him. Worse. Confess that he was, despite all things written and said, a nice man.

Merida wouldn't love him so much otherwise.

She didn't doubt that seeing his wife, in labour, pleading for love and for this marriage to survive, would manipulate him into agreeing.

He might even mean it for a while.

But he did not love her the way she loved him, with this all-consuming, burning love, and she did not want to be placated with crumbs.

'Go,' Merida said. 'Let me get some sleep.'

'I'm not going home.'

'Then go and spend some time with your father.'

'It's midnight.'

'I doubt he cares about the time when it might be his last night on earth.' And then she begged him. *'Go.'*

And he had no choice but to leave. 'I'll be back at six—unless there are any changes.'

Ethan spoke to the nurse and checked she had his direct number, but then, instead of going to see his father, he headed over to the freezing park.

He had had so many plans for tonight.

But Merida was right. They weren't ready for the baby yet.

He looked up at the cold grey sky and the endless fall of snow and knew that time was close to running out for his father.

It was the middle of the night, and no doubt he was doped up to the eyeballs, sleeping. But what Merida had said about it possibly being Jobe's last night on earth made him brave enough to try.

He sent a text.

Hey, Merida has been admitted. Nothing expected till tomorrow.

Good news! How she?

He'd missed out the 'is', but the fact that he could be so doped up and still text had Ethan in awe.

Asleep. Do you want some company?

Ethan hit 'send' and held his breath as he awaited the reply.

Sounds good.

Ethan entered his father's suite. There was no mistaking it was a hospital room now, but Jobe was sitting up in bed.

'How is she?' he asked.

'It's very early days, apparently. She's asleep—they told her to rest.' He took a seat by his father's bed.

'Her friend gets here tomorrow?' he asked.

'Naomi.' Ethan nodded. 'I'll send a driver to the airport. I'd better be here for the main show!'

Jobe gave a small laugh.

'Were you there when we were born?'

'I was.' Jobe nodded. 'But not so much after.' He turned and looked at his youngest son. 'I regret that.'

'You love work…' Ethan said.

'Oh, I do love work—it's not the time spent there I regret.'

'You can't have both,' Ethan quipped, and then he stopped trying to halt his father. 'What do you regret?'

Jobe said nothing.

So finally Ethan did.

'I know that things must have been difficult with Mom.' He looked at his father's fading dark eyes and wished he could be here for longer. 'I don't blame you for what happened with you and Meghan…' He swallowed back tears. 'I did when I was younger, because I missed Meghan, and I blew it up in my head that it was all your fault, but I…'

'There was no affair.'

The world seemed to stop spinning and then Jobe spoke on.

'Meghan came and told me that she couldn't stand back any longer—that she had no choice but to leave.'

'Why?'

'Because of how your mother treated you boys.'

The world had still ceased spinning.

'She left you on the sofa once—face-down. She left Abe alone in the bath… Meghan simply couldn't do it any more.'

He stared at his father and remembered being hauled out of the car and into the shower, and he knew then that he had almost died.

'So why did you let the world think there was an affair?'

'That was your mother's doing at first. But then came the accident, and it was easier to let you think she was perfect.'

'She wasn't, though.'

'No.'

To Elizabeth Devereux her babies had been mere

toys. Decoys. Dragged out to smile for the cameras and then ignored the moment they weren't around.

But, like all true narcissists, she had loved her place in the sun and any threat to it had been quickly eliminated.

Like Meghan.

She had let the world think the nanny a cheat. And when Jobe had wanted a divorce, and threatened to expose the truth about they way she treated his children, she had simply run towards the sun with no thought of the chaos she'd left behind her.

Ethan had lost two mothers in one month—the mother who'd given birth to him but also, worse, the woman who had truly cared for him.

'I said to Merida that I would go to my grave not telling you…'

'Merida already knows?'

'Of course she does.'

'So why hasn't she said anything?'

'The same reason as me,' Jobe said. 'You don't want to hurt those you love. And I *do* love you, son.'

'I love you too.'

'Now, go and be with your wife.'

He wanted to be with Merida, but he wanted to be here too, and Jobe must have seen indecision dart in his eyes.

'I'm not going anywhere yet,' he said.

'Are you sure?'

'I want to know what you have.'

'A grandchild,' Ethan said. 'And you'll be a grandfather. Do *you* know what we're having?'

'No.' Jobe shook his head.

'Liar.'

'I don't.' He nodded, as if gesturing to something. 'Open that.'

'What?'

'The drawer.'

Ethan did so, and there was an envelope.

'I had Merida's OB write it down, just in case…'

Ethan wiped away tears and smiled. The world had gone back to spinning, and yet it felt different now. Precious and valuable, and vital and time-poor—as the world was when you were in love.

'It's not a sham, Dad. I want you to know that. I love her…'

'I know you do. I knew the night I saw her.'

'How?'

'You took her to the bridge. You were looking out for her even in the contract…' He gave his son a smile. 'Lots of things. But really the fact that you married her, Ethan.'

'I'm going to be there for Merida and the baby,' Ethan told him.

'And Abe,' Jobe said. 'I worry about him.'

'Abe's fine.'

'No.' Jobe shook his head. 'I shan't live to see him sorted, I know that, but tell me you'll look out for him?'

'I doubt he'll appreciate it,' Ethan said, but then he was serious. 'Always.'

'Does Merida know that you love her yet?'

'Once the baby is here…'

'No,' Jobe said. 'Tell her *now.*'

'She needs to sleep.'

'Why would anyone want to sleep lonely when they could be finding out they're loved? I'm damned glad you woke me. Now, go.' He waved him away. 'I need my sleep. I've got my grandchild to meet.'

Merida stirred as Ethan came in.

Ethan had been crying.

The artist had had little colour in his palette when he'd created this masterpiece, but apart from the deep red of his lips this morning crimson rimmed his eyes. And she rather knew that it was private and that he might not want her to see.

'How's your father?' Merida asked, filled with dread, because she did not want her baby born on the day Jobe died.

More than that, she did not want Jobe to die!

'Hanging in there,' Ethan said. 'He sends his best wishes.'

'That's nice.'

'What's happening?' He looked at all the machines, rather than look at her, because he was trying to summon up the courage for the rather important thing he had to say.

'I'm being examined at six.'

Ethan nodded and then put his hand into the deep pocket of his coat. 'Here.'

He dropped a black pouch on the bed and she stared at it for a time.

'I was going to give you this…' He was about to

say *when the baby was here*, or perhaps lie and say he had been going to give her this last night, but the truth was he didn't know when the time was right to admit to love. 'I've been carrying it around for some time.'

She opened the pouch and into her palm slid a huge red-gold egg.

'I had Khalid source it.'

Merida swallowed.

'It took a while—amber is rare in Al-Zahan.'

It was magnificent. There were wide streaks of gold and a dragonfly, deep within.

'It's the colour of your hair,' Ethan said. 'One of my favourite things.'

Their amulet.

'I knew we didn't need help with the fertility part, but...' And then he hesitated, because maybe they didn't need help with the other thing either. 'I know that I love you.'

'Please don't just say that.'

'I'm not.' Ethan shook his head. 'In fact, I didn't *want* to love you.'

'Why not?'

'Because then you'd leave.' He finally admitted the truth. The gnawing of fear he'd grown up with. 'But I've loved you for a very long time.'

'When?' Merida asked. 'When did you know that you did?'

'The morning I first left you in the coffee shop.'

She looked at him. There was anger sweeping

over her, for all the pain they'd been through, and yet it was doused by the utter relief that truth brought.

'And I knew again on that opening night, when the curtains parted on the stage and you weren't there.'

'So why couldn't you tell me?'

'It was easier to pretend to myself you were a gold-digger. And you did a pretty convincing act for a while.' He met her eyes. 'I'm putting you back to work as soon as the baby's old enough, Ms Merida Cartwright! You're an actress indeed.'

'Do you blame me for pretending to hate you?'

'No.'

'You spoke over and over about when we were through.'

'Because I believed that we would be.'

He'd simply believed that one day he'd wake up and she'd be gone. Like his mother. Like Meghan.

'I'm like my father,' Ethan said. 'And it used to terrify me, but now I could not be prouder of him. I know why he broke up with Chantelle—because I'm the same. I didn't want to give you the hard times that I knew were about to come.'

'But I *want* to be here,' Merida said. 'I want to be with your dad. I want *all* of you, Ethan.'

The whole thing. The good and the bad and the precious bits in between, when the world just bumped along with love at their side.

She held on to their amulet as she was examined and told that it was time to push. She was ready—more than ready—for their baby to be here.

It was intense work, but Ethan brought energy to her, and although she could have done it alone, Merida didn't have to.

And she didn't have to be brave or strong. She just felt as if she was as their baby inched its way into the world.

It was hard, gritty work—and then there was the reward.

'Black hair,' Ethan said. 'It's a Devereux.'

'It hurts enough to be one!'

He smiled as she trumped him, and then looked at her with black eyes that were always dark. Yet, like the night, there were some darknesses more beautiful than others. Some less lonely. And some you never forgot.

'Come on, Merida,' he told her.

Merida breathed in deeply and gathered her strength. And pushed when she wasn't sure she knew how to. She pushed not against but *towards* love.

And then she pushed again.

And again.

'One more,' Ethan said.

And then they met the sum of their love.

Long-limbed, she unfurled, jittery and indignant, flailing at the bright, noisy world.

And Ethan watched as Merida held her as if she would never let her go.

Of course he could not remember all those days so long ago when his mother had discarded him with such ease. But he knew in his soul that it was a hurt his child would never know.

And then he held her himself.

She wore a little white cap and stared up at him with huge dark eyes, and Ethan was besotted with his little girl.

He looked over to his stunning wife.

'For a one-night stand, I did very well for myself,' he said, and smiled.

'It wasn't a one-night stand,' Merida refuted. 'I just happened to sleep with you on our first date.'

It *had* been a date, Ethan thought as they kissed, their baby between them. Their first date. And it would not be their last.

'I'm going to spend the rest of our lives making up for lost time.'

'It was hell,' Merida said, 'but I still loved every minute.'

'And me,' Ethan said.

After all, she had awoken his heart.

EPILOGUE

'MY FATHER WANTS to come down to see her.'

'Don't be daft.' Merida sat up in the bed. 'We'll take her up to see him.'

'I said that, but he insists on coming down.' Ethan hesitated. 'He wants photos.'

'Of course.'

'No.' Ethan was quite sure she didn't understand. 'He wants the happy family shot.'

Merida lay back on the pillow and gave an exhausted half-laugh.

Ethan had told her that he knew now that there had been no affair with Meghan. And he'd told her about the hell of those family photos, being forced to smile when his heart was damaged almost to broken.

Then he'd told her *his* child would never be exposed to that.

'Ethan…'

'I know.' He looked at his wife, who was beyond exhausted. 'No photos.'

And of all the things she knew of her husband, she knew he was doing his hardest to get this fatherhood thing right. That, even when his heart was both bursting with love and splitting with grief, he was doing his best to do right by her.

'Of course he can have his photo with Ava—and if he wants a family shot then so do I. I'll ask if there's someone who can come and do something with my hair, and—'

'I can do it.'

Naomi had just come from the airport. Her suitcases were stacked in a corner and she had popped in to glimpse her new charge.

'I'll help you get ready for the photos and then—'

A gruff voice interrupted the chatter. 'There's no need for all that.'

Merida looked up as Jobe Devereux was wheeled in.

He wore a silk dressing gown and his salt and pepper hair was immaculate. There was not a drip or machine in sight, and Merida could absolutely guess the effort he had gone to for this.

This was the amazing family she had married into.

'So when do I get to meet her?' Jobe asked.

'Now!' Merida smiled.

Ava was there, quiet in her little Perspex crib, so quiet that Jobe hadn't seen her.

And now Merida watched as Ethan went over, pulled back the little blanket and picked up their tiny daughter.

She was a shock of dark hair and bunched-up pink legs, with name tags around her ankles and flailing arms, and she let out an angry cry.

But Ethan hushed her. He held her tight in his arms as he tucked her blanket around her, and he was just so tender with her that it brought tears to Merida's eyes.

'Meet Ava,' Ethan said, and handed the tiny little girl to his father.

Merida stopped even trying to fight the tears as three generations met. Oh, she wanted photos. A hundred of them. She wanted these precious moments captured.

The way Ethan proudly looked on as his father embraced his granddaughter and told them things they could never have known without him being here.

'Those blue eyes will be black by New Year,' Jobe said, never taking his eyes from Ava. 'Abe's took four weeks to turn, and Ethan's three...'

And Jobe passed on more of those tiny details that mattered and that only someone who loved you knew.

'I'm going to head off.' Naomi gave Merida a kiss as a porter came for her cases.

'Thanks for coming,' Merida said. 'Your room's all ready...'

'Don't worry about me,' Naomi said. 'I'm going to sleep off this jet-lag and be ready for when you bring Ava home.'

It was a wondrous, exhausting, exhilarating afternoon.

Even Abe appeared, minus Candice. He didn't stay long.

And when the day was done—when Ava had been fed and changed—he took their baby and wrapped her in a cream shawl, laid her safely down in her crib. He stroked her with a feather-light trace of her brow, soothing her to sleep.

'I can't wait to get you both home,' Ethan said as he watched his daughter prepare for her first night's sleep.

It would be Jobe's home that they'd sleep in for now, but that didn't daunt Ethan any more. New memories were being made and would soon line the walls.

'See this?' he said to Merida, and took out his phone. 'It's going on the wall.'

It was a gorgeous picture of a bride and groom, kissing on a rather gorgeous bridge.

'Our wedding day…' Merida smiled.

'I loved you then,' Ethan told her. 'And I love you now. I always shall.'

They had found their love.

* * * * *

If you enjoyed
The Innocent's Shock Pregnancy
by Carol Marinelli
you're sure to enjoy these other
One Night With Consequences stories!

The Sheikh's Shock Child
by Susan Stephens
Crowned for the Sheikh's Baby
by Sharon Kendrick
The Italian's One-Night Consequence
by Cathy Williams
Princess's Nine-Month Secret
by Kate Hewitt
Consequence of the Tycoon's Revenge
by Trish Morey

Available now!

COMING NEXT MONTH FROM

HARLEQUIN

Presents®

Available November 20, 2018

#3673 THE ITALIAN'S INHERITED MISTRESS
by Lynne Graham

Isla has escaped to her recently inherited Sicilian villa, and the last person she expects to see is the billionaire who changed her life irrevocably. Alissandru wants what's rightfully his—Isla's inheritance. But what he wants more is Isla...back in his bed!

#3674 MARRIED FOR HIS ONE-NIGHT HEIR
Secret Heirs of Billionaires
by Jennifer Hayward

Santo's stunned to see Giovanna again. Why, after that one forbidden night, did she leave? But when Gia reveals their secret consequence, the Italian will claim his son—and Gia as his wife!

#3675 CLAIMING HIS CHRISTMAS WIFE
Conveniently Wed!
by Dani Collins

After their marriage ended in heartbreak, Travis never wanted to see Imogen again. But to avoid a scandal, they must agree to a temporary reconciliation—leaving Travis tempted to reclaim his wife...for good!

#3676 BOUND BY THEIR CHRISTMAS BABY
Christmas Seductions
by Clare Connelly

To legitimize his son, Gabe knows he must marry Abby—the innocent beauty he shared a steamy festive night with! But can their marriage be in name only, or will red-hot chemistry take over?

HPCNM1118RA

#3677 AN INNOCENT, A SEDUCTION, A SECRET
One Night With Consequences
by Abby Green

When Seb spies Edie's talent for lavish interior decoration, he makes an irresistible job offer—spend the festive season decorating his opulent home! But soon, Edie becomes the sensual gift Seb wishes to unwrap...

#3678 THE BILLIONAIRE'S CHRISTMAS CINDERELLA
by Carol Marinelli

Abe Devereux is famed for his cold heart. So meeting Naomi, who's determined to see the good in him, is a novelty. But will seducing her be his biggest risk, or his greatest chance of redemption?

#3679 PREGNANT BY THE DESERT KING
by Susan Stephens

Lucy is shocked by Tadj's royal revelation: Lucy is carrying the baby of a desert king! Tadj will secure his heir, but can Lucy accept his scandalous solution—that she share his royal bed?

#3680 THE VIRGIN'S SICILIAN PROTECTOR
by Chantelle Shaw

Hired to keep heiress Ariana safe, wealthy bodyguard Santino is intrigued by her hidden vulnerability. Their sexual tension is electric! And when Santino discovers just how innocent Ariana is, resisting her temptation becomes an impossible challenge...

YOU CAN FIND MORE INFORMATION ON UPCOMING HARLEQUIN® TITLES, FREE EXCERPTS AND MORE AT WWW.HARLEQUIN.COM.

HPCNM1118RB

Get 4 FREE REWARDS!

We'll send you 2 FREE Books
<u>plus</u> 2 FREE Mystery Gifts.

Harlequin Presents® books feature a sensational and sophisticated world of international romance where sinfully tempting heroes ignite passion.

FREE
Value Over
$20

YES! Please send me 2 FREE Harlequin Presents® novels and my 2 FREE gifts (gifts are worth about $10 retail). After receiving them, if I don't wish to receive any more books, I can return the shipping statement marked "cancel." If I don't cancel, I will receive 6 brand-new novels every month and be billed just $4.55 each for the regular-print edition or $5.55 each for the larger-print edition in the U.S., or $5.49 each for the regular-print edition or $5.99 each for the larger-print edition in Canada. That's a savings of at least 11% off the cover price! It's quite a bargain! Shipping and handling is just 50¢ per book in the U.S. and 75¢ per book in Canada*. I understand that accepting the 2 free books and gifts places me under no obligation to buy anything. I can always return a shipment and cancel at any time. The free books and gifts are mine to keep no matter what I decide.

Choose one: ☐ **Harlequin Presents®**
Regular-Print
(106/306 HDN GMYX)

☐ **Harlequin Presents®**
Larger-Print
(176/376 HDN GMYX)

Name (please print)

Address   Apt. #

City   State/Province   Zip/Postal Code

Mail to the **Reader Service:**
IN U.S.A.: P.O. Box 1341, Buffalo, NY 14240-8531
IN CANADA: P.O. Box 603, Fort Erie, Ontario L2A 5X3

Want to try two free books from another series? Call 1-800-873-8635 or visit www.ReaderService.com.

*Terms and prices subject to change without notice. Prices do not include applicable taxes. Sales tax applicable in N.Y. Canadian residents will be charged applicable taxes. Offer not valid in Quebec. This offer is limited to one order per household. Books received may not be as shown. Not valid for current subscribers to Harlequin Presents books. All orders subject to approval. Credit or debit balances in a customer's account(s) may be offset by any other outstanding balance owed by or to the customer. Please allow 4 to 6 weeks for delivery. Offer available while quantities last.

Your Privacy—The Reader Service is committed to protecting your privacy. Our Privacy Policy is available online at www.ReaderService.com or upon request from the Reader Service. We make a portion of our mailing list available to reputable third parties that offer products we believe may interest you. If you prefer that we not exchange your name with third parties, or if you wish to clarify or modify your communication preferences, please visit us at www.ReaderService.com/consumerschoice or write to us at Reader Service Preference Service, P.O. Box 9062, Buffalo, NY 14240-9062. Include your complete name and address.

HP18

SPECIAL EXCERPT FROM

HARLEQUIN

Presents®

*Santo's stunned to see Giovanna again. Why, after
that one forbidden night, did she leave? But when Gia
reveals their secret consequence, the Italian will claim
his son—and Gia as his wife!*

*Read on for a sneak preview of
Jennifer Hayward's next story,*
Married for a One-Night Consequence.

He set his glass down with a clatter. "I am his *father.* I
have missed three years of his life. You think a *weekend
pass* is going to suffice? A few dips in the Caribbean as he
learns to swim?" He fixed his gaze on hers. "I want *every
day* with him. I want it *all.*"

"What else can we do?" she queried helplessly. "You
live in New York and I live here. Leo is settled and
happy. A limited custody arrangement is the only realistic
proposition."

"It is *not* a viable proposition." His low growl made
her jump. "That's not going to work, Gia."

She eyed him warily. "Which part?"

"All of it." He waved a Rolex-clad wrist at her. "I
have a proposal for you. It's the only one on the table,
nonnegotiable on all points. Take it or leave it."

The wariness written across her face intensified. "Which is?"

"We do what's in the best interests of our child. You marry me, we create a life together in New York and give Leo the family he deserves."

Don't miss
Married for a One-Night Consequence,
available December 2018 wherever
Harlequin Presents® books and ebooks are sold.

www.Harlequin.com

Copyright © 2018 by Jennifer Hayward

HPEXP1118

HARLEQUIN *Presents*®

Coming next month—a festive trio just in time
for the holidays!

Claiming His Christmas Wife by Dani Collins

Part of the Conveniently Wed! miniseries

When Imogen faints in the cold New York snow,
Travis is called to his ex-wife's very public rescue!
But, with a deal *just* for Christmas, will he be able
to let Imogen go a second time?

Bound by Their Christmas Baby by Clare Connelly

Part of the Christmas Seductions miniseries

When brooding bachelor Gabe learns Abby is his business
rival's daughter, he's furious. So what will he do when she
returns the following Christmas with their secret baby?

The Billionaire's Christmas Cinderella by Carol Marinelli

Tycoon Abe is overwhelmed by the potency of his
undeniable connection with Naomi. Now he wants
this shy Cinderella between his sheets by Christmas!

Available December 2018

HPBPA1118